G000153511

Þ
Þen

by
Evelyn James

A Clara Fitzgerald Mystery
Book 6

Red Raven Publications
2017

Other Books in
The Clara Fitzgerald Series

Chapter One

It was late February 1921. Clara Fitzgerald, Brighton's first female private detective, had spent January recuperating from a bout of influenza she had caught in London during her last case. Now she was feeling much better and was eager to get back to work. The sun was shining as she made her way to her office for the first time in over a month. Clara rented a couple of rooms over a draper's shop to serve as a business address. It was preferable to interviewing clients at her own house though, invariably, they found their way to her home address at some point. Clara had come to accept that completely isolating her work as a detective from her private life was virtually impossible.

There was a hint of spring in the air. Clara was glad of it. Winter made her morose, and this winter had been particularly challenging after the incidents at Berkeley Square and the sad (but completely natural) death of her elderly client Miss Sampford. Clara being so poorly had not helped her mood either; there had been moments when her brother Tommy and their maid Annie had been quite concerned about her. A doctor had been called one Saturday afternoon and had insisted on Clara taking some foul medicine, which made her feel infinitely worse, though, quite remarkably, she actually improved afterwards.

Unlike Annie and Tommy, Clara had never considered herself in any danger of dying. She was quite convinced she was made of sterner stuff, and no amount of sneezing, coughing or feverish temperatures was going to change that.

Clara waved to Mr Sloane who ran the draper's shop. He was sweeping his front step to remove mud traipsed onto it by his customers. He gave her a grin and announced he was pleased to see her back. If you didn't know, you never would have guessed from Mr Sloane's crisp, English accent, that he was actually a Russian Jew who had fled to Britain from the anti-Jewish pogroms in Russia during the 1880s. Mr Sloane knew what it was like to be an outsider and considered 'abnormal', it was why he had such sympathy for a woman trying to strike up a business in a man's world, and also why he had originally rented Clara the rooms above his shop at a foolishly low price. Even now, when Clara was making a respectable income from her work, he refused her pleas to raise the rent. Mr Sloane was just happy that Clara was there.

Clara had a separate door to her rooms over the shop; it led straight onto a narrow staircase. She unlocked it, collected a handful of letters from the doormat, and hastened upstairs to make a cup of tea and get to work. Clara was just opening the first letter, which appeared to be an advertisement of some sort, when Mr Sloane hurried in.

"Ah, I forgot. There is a lady who has been coming every Monday to try and see you. I told her you were quite ill and I could not say when you would be back at work. She stated she would keep trying. Today, you see, is Monday."

Clara smiled at the draper.

"Thank you Mr Sloane, so I should expect a visitor shortly?"

"I imagine so, yes," Mr Sloane gave her another nod

and started to leave. "Oh, my wife made some shortbread. Please join us at 11 o'clock for a tea break and partake of some."

Clara assured Mr Sloane she would and watched the draper leave. She went back to her post. There was a short letter from Edward Sampford, the brother of her last client, thanking her for all her hard work. It seemed a rather formal, bittersweet letter and made Clara feel rather despondent again. She was relieved when the doorbell went.

Clara hurried down the stairs, and opened the door to the street, to see Mrs Wilton standing before her. Mrs Wilton was one of Clara's very first clients. She was a remarkably superstitious woman who had been tricked into believing her dead husband had left buried treasure by a fraudulent medium. In Clara's opinion, Mrs Wilton was a sweet, but rather silly, woman who had struggled to cope with life since her husband's death in the war. Seeing her on the doorstep now, filled Clara with a sense of foreboding.

"Mrs Wilton," she said in a welcoming tone to mask her dread.

"I am so glad you are in, my dear. Are you quite well? You look exceptionally pale, but then perhaps that is how girls want to look these days. Dear me…" Mrs Wilton tailed off, looking flustered. She was not a woman who coped well with problems.

"Would you care to come in for a cup of tea?" Clara asked. "Then you can tell me all about what is worrying you."

"Yes, yes that would be good."

Mrs Wilton followed Clara upstairs and sat patiently in a chair, while Clara made a pot of tea.

"My, my. It hardly seems a year ago I was last in this office!" she said, glancing up at the portrait of Clara's father on the wall.

"Is your son well?" Clara asked a little anxiously. Until last year, Mrs Wilton had thought her son had also died in the war. Clara had been able to reunite them.

"Oh he is fine, dear. This is not about me, you understand. I am here on behalf of a friend."

Clara wasn't sure whether to relax at this news or to be more concerned. She set a cup of tea before Mrs Wilton.

"Why doesn't your friend come herself?"

"It is very difficult. To be honest with you, Clara, it took considerable time to persuade her to let me come on her behalf. She is very worried," Mrs Wilton took a long sip of tea. "I think she was rather mortified at the idea of calling on the services of a private detective. She considered it rather distasteful. But it was either that or inform the police."

Now Clara was curious.

"Has a crime been committed?"

"I should say so!" Mrs Wilton tutted. "Mind you, it isn't public knowledge yet, though I expect to see a newspaper report on the matter any day now."

Mrs Wilton was being her usual, infuriatingly cryptic, self.

"Perhaps you can explain exactly what has happened?" Clara pressed her.

"Why yes!" Mrs Wilton smiled. "Poison pen letters, my dear! You know what I mean?"

"Yes. Letters that insult or offend the recipient, or insinuate they have committed some sin. Usually anonymous, and very distasteful."

"Well, there has been a spate of them around the area I live. Quite a number of people have received these disgusting things. In fact, I got one myself," Mrs Wilton unclipped her handbag and produced a letter. "It is really quite awful, but I kept it, as I realised it was evidence."

Clara unfolded the crumpled letter. It had clearly been screwed up into a ball at some point, perhaps before Mrs Wilton had realised its value. The handwriting was very neat and clear, which made its rather blunt statements all the worse.

Dear Mrs Wilton

We know your husband is not really dead but living in London with a floozy. Your condoning of this shameful behaviour not only makes you despicable but foolish. We also know the man you claim is your son is really your lover, who you have moved into your home to fill the void in your hollow, miserable life. You are a sorry excuse for a woman and we spit on you! You are a disgrace to the neighbourhood and the sooner others realise this, the better!

The letter had no signature and finished abruptly.

"Of course, I laughed at it," Mrs Wilton said, looking distinctly like she had not laughed at all. Mrs Wilton was a very sensitive soul.

"It is all lies," Clara said calmly.

"Absolutely!" Mrs Wilton rallied a touch. "But it struck a nerve. I began to wonder if other people were thinking the same thing. For a time I was a little nervous about leaving the house. I looked at my neighbours and the people I met in the street and found myself wondering if they were behind it. Then, finally, I confided in a friend, and she said she had also received an awful letter. A little prudent investigation revealed that at least ten of our neighbours had also received such notes, some much worse than others. We decided to hold a meeting about it. Everyone came to my friend, Mrs Hampton's, house. Well, no one really seemed to have much of an idea who was behind the notes, they were just very upset. Mrs Hampton suggested we speak to the police, but everyone was rather reluctant, as some of the letters have come a little too close to revealing real secrets.

"That was when I found myself looking at Mrs Prinner. She is a little older than my son, married, with two children. A nice woman, who had received the most ghastly letter, and the expression on her face as she sat listening to the discussion! Well, I just knew that she knew more than she was letting on! After the meeting I took her to one side. I am on friendly terms with her. And I mentioned that I sensed she knew something more than the rest of us. She admitted she suspected she knew who the writer of the letter was! But she would not tell me anymore. Finally I persuaded Mrs Hampton that we must get some help. Since our meeting another five letters have been delivered. One went to Mrs Summerton who is eight months pregnant. It gave her such a shock a doctor had to be called and we all thought she would lose the baby. At some point, Clara, these letters are going to do more than upset people. They are going to cause real harm!"

"I quite agree," Clara had continued to look at the note as Mrs Wilton spoke. "Poison pen letters are a nasty business. That nothing bad has happened because of them already is pure luck, but something must be done."

"Then, might I invite you to a meeting of those who have received these letters, tonight, at Mrs Hampton's?" Mrs Wilton held out a slip of paper, with an address written on it, to Clara.

"I shall come," Clara took the paper. "And it would be most helpful if I could have every letter that remains to study for patterns in handwriting and such. I promise that no word I read will be shared with anyone and you can vouch for my discretion."

"Yes, I can. That is precisely why I came to you. We don't want a lot of policemen sticking their noses into our business. Far better to engage a sensible woman who knows when to hold her tongue. This must be resolved soon, Clara!"

"I shall do my best," Clara assured her. "Do you happen to have any thoughts on who might be behind this?"

Mrs Wilton sighed.

"I wish I did, but no, I can't think of anyone who would be so awful. Or perhaps I am too trusting?" Mrs Wilton tapped her fingers unconsciously on the side of the desk. "Why would someone do such a thing?"

"Usually, such letter writers are very bitter people,

filled with a verbal bile that spills out onto paper. Because they are unhappy they tend to want to lash out at people they perceive as being happy, or as having more than them. Yes, jealousy plays a part too. Behind the pen is a person who is very sad, lonely and dysfunctional. In many regards they deserve our sympathy."

"Hmph! I think not Clara!" Mrs Wilton said stoutly. "I have no time to feel sorry for such vile people. Just find them and stop them."

"I shall endeavour," Clara promised.

When Mrs Wilton had gone, Clara found a magnifying glass and took a closer look at the letter she had been handed. The writing was in black ink, the letters had a gentle loop to them that suggested a well-educated hand. The spelling was precise and there was no indication of an error. Each word had been written with care, the letters well-defined, with distinct spaces between words to make the letter easy to read. This was not a person who wanted their writing misunderstood. The paper was of good quality and from a brand Clara had seen stocked in the Post Office. There was a watermark of a pelican impressed into the paper. She could see it when she held the letter up to the light. But all that really told her, was that the writer liked to use good paper, and they had enough spare money to not concern themselves about using that same paper for such a petty and pointless task as poison pen letters.

On the other hand, the information in the letter was mundane. Everyone knew Mrs Wilton had lost her husband in the war, and it was certainly no secret that her long-lost son had returned last year. The pen writer had clearly wanted to put their own spin on two innocent circumstances, but there was no basis in truth for the claims – Clara knew that for a fact, having investigated the deaths of Mrs Wilton's husband and son, herself, as part of the case. She had not only proved that Mr Wilton had died at the Front, as his wife had been told, but that her son had actually survived. No, the letter writer was making spurious claims to fulfil a need for spite. But what of the other letters? Could it be that the writer had stumbled across genuine secrets they now wished to reveal? It would be interesting to see what the remaining letters told her about the person behind them. Were they just being spiteful, or could they have access to damaging secrets about certain residents in Brighton? If so, it was only a matter of time before someone was hurt because of these letters. Clara looked at the piece of paper grimly. What a terrible business, she thought to herself. Then her stomach gave a rumble to remind her she had missed breakfast. Mrs Sloane's shortbread was calling. It was never good to contemplate a new case on an empty belly.

Chapter Two

Clara locked up her office at four o'clock and headed home for tea. Her mind was still on the poison pen letters and the messages they contained. There was something about poison pen writers that brought a surge of anger into Clara's chest and stomach. Maybe it was the fact they were acting anonymously, causing harm without ever showing themselves. It was such a cowardly thing to do.

She walked home in the dusk. The streets were still busy with people. There were at least another couple of working hours to be squeezed out of the day. She passed a newspaper boy hawking the evening addition, and bought a copy to read the headlines. Brighton was quiet, news-wise, as was usual in the seaside resort. There had been a couple of break-ins of empty houses and the Brighton Pavilion had been vandalised by boys throwing stones at the façade yet again, but there was little to truly worry about. Clara folded the paper under her arm and hurried home.

Annie baked scones on a Monday. Though dry fruit and sugar were still scarce in the shops after the war, Annie always managed to present her scones with butter and a small portion of jam. The jam was often of unusual flavours, like quince or gooseberry, and a good deal sharper than the jam Clara remembered from pre-war, but she had grown to like it and doubted she would ever be able to happily consume sugary jam again. Clara looked forward to her scones, followed later in the evening by a minced meat pie made from the remains of the Sunday roast, and served with potatoes. Clara reflected this was probably why she was still failing to achieve the svelte figure that was all the rage among young women at the moment.

Clara opened the front door of her house and found herself face-to-face with Inspector Park-Coombs of the Brighton constabulary. Park-Coombs was a man in his forties, whose role as Inspector had taken its toll and made him look a good few years older than he really was. His hair was greying at the sides and there were even hints of grey in his moustache, which he clearly took great pride over. Today, as he stood in Clara's hallway, he looked even more harassed than normal.

"Inspector," Clara said in surprise. "Have you been waiting long?"

"A few minutes, that's all," the inspector said carelessly. "I need to speak to you Clara, it is quite urgent."

Clara could see that. The Inspector did not usually call on her for a casual chat.

"Come into the parlour," Clara showed the inspector into her cosy front room, where a fire was burning in the grate and the air smelt of fresh polish and the aroma of toast left-over from breakfast. She indicated a chair for the Inspector to sit in.

"You look done in," she told him, as she sat down herself. "Something must be the matter."

The inspector rubbed his hand over his eyes wearily.

"I feel done in," he admitted. "These are bad times, Clara, for the police, that is. Do you remember that episode we had last summer when Billy 'Razor' Brown escaped from our police cells?"

Clara could hardly forget. Billy had come after her for

the sole purpose of shutting her up.

"Yes," she said nervously, wondering if another criminal had escaped from Brighton's police cells.

"At the time I was naturally concerned. But the more I looked into the matter, the more I was deeply troubled. Billy didn't break out of his cell. I am certain someone opened the door for him."

"And that someone may have been a policeman?"

The Inspector nodded solemnly.

"There have been other signs. Odd things. Reports missing vital information. Evidence going missing. Don't get me wrong, policemen don't make the best clerks, and a few of my lads definitely struggle with a typewriter, not to mention filing. But this is something more than just careless mistakes."

Clara merely nodded. She understood that feeling of a nagging doubt in the pit of the stomach. Some called it intuition, or even paranoia, she felt it was the thing that divided a good detective from a mediocre one.

"Do you have a suspect in mind?"

"That's just the thing, Clara. I have become so suspicious of everyone. But, the real problem is, the more I poke around the more the traitor goes to ground to cover their tracks. An Inspector can only dabble so much before his constables start to wonder what he is about, and the villain among them grows nervous and starts to take precautions."

"I see," Clara said, sensing where this was leading.

"I need an outsider with a bit of sense to investigate for me. I thought of you because your presence is already familiar at the police station and would not seem out of place. You can pretend to be working on other cases, when actually you will be poking around on my behalf."

"This is a very serious matter, Inspector."

"I know. I suspect one of my officers has become mixed up with London gangsters. It is the only way to explain Billy Brown's miraculous escape. I dislike the thought of policemen being bribed by thugs and rogues, but that is what it looks like."

Clara hesitated a moment. Was she up to this challenge? When she last was involved with organised crime her life had come into serious peril, but at least then she had felt she had the back-up of the police. Now who would she turn to if she needed help?

"I know I am asking a lot," Inspector Park-Coombs filled the silence. "But I am not sure who else to turn to. Discretion is vital. I could report this to my superiors, but the scandal of an official investigation would be devastating for the police. You are probably aware that the British constabulary is not held in as high a regard by the public as it used to be?"

Clara was aware. The police strikes of 1918 and 1919 had undermined the Force, and left the government surly towards any boy in blue causing trouble. Even a whiff of corruption among Brighton's policemen would do a great deal of harm, not least to those who were innocent of the crime.

"Have you any suggestions about where I might begin?" she said at last.

"Two, actually. I have written down the names of the three men on duty in the station at the time Billy Brown escaped, they might be worth investigating closely. But, I suggest your best way into this mess, is to investigate Constable Brompton's unfortunate accident."

"Constable Brompton?" Clara racked her brain for the name. "Oh, there was something in the papers. Wasn't he hit by a drunk driver while patrolling one night?"

"That is the story we told the press. To be honest, up until recently, it was the story I believed as well. But I started to have my doubts about it when I realised Brompton's mishap coincided with the first signs I can find of something being wrong at my station. It happened around the time evidence started to go missing and reports were being written in a misleading fashion. I started to think perhaps Brompton had stumbled onto something."

"Brompton survived the accident, didn't he?"

"Barely. His skull was fractured and both legs were broken. He recovered, but he could never be a bobby again. I managed to see that he got a job at the hospital in their clerical department. He spends his days filing patient reports. He can manage that, fortunately, but ask him to do anything more taxing and, well... you'll see."

"When would be the best time to pay him a call?"

"He works a regular twelve hour shift at the hospital on weekdays. Begins at eight in the morning. He lives at home with his parents the rest of the time."

"And you are really certain there is a crooked policeman in your midst?"

Inspector Park-Coombs raised his hands in a motion of defeat.

"If you could prove otherwise, I would be most grateful," he smiled sadly. "Somehow, I think you won't."

"I shall look into it Inspector, you can count on me."

"Thank you Clara."

"Now, won't you stay for tea?"

"No, the wife is expecting me," Park-Coombs rose with a groan. "She knows something is up, so I dare not be late and worry her. I haven't told her anything, naturally."

"Naturally, Inspector," Clara escorted him to the door. "I'll do my best for you."

"Thank you," the Inspector took his coat off a peg and rummaged in a pocket. "Here is that list of names I mentioned."

"Take care, Inspector," Clara said as he went down the garden path. She closed the door behind him, a strange sensation of the world tilting off-kilter coming over her. If you couldn't trust the police, where were you?

Chapter Three

Around seven o'clock, Clara made her way to the address Mrs Wilton had given her. She found herself in front of a red brick terrace house with a very neat garden and a gravel path. A discreetly placed porcelain gnome smiled at her from a patch of crocuses just coming into bloom, as she walked to the door. She rang the bell and was soon greeted by a thin woman in a navy blue smock dress. She had very long hands with narrow fingers, in which she took both of Clara's hands and welcomed her warmly, before ushering her to the back parlour.

The room was already crowded with quite a selection of people. Mrs Wilton had said that at least fifteen people had received letters (herself and Mrs Hampton included), and it seemed nearly every recipient had come that night to find out what Brighton's very own Miss Fitzgerald was going to do about the matter. That meant the small back room was crammed with people. Mrs Hampton had done a valiant job of finding them all seats, though she had had to beg chairs off neighbours and a couple of the participants were 'making do' with squatting on foot stools. Clara surveyed the assortment of worried faces and felt a pang of nerves. Fifteen faces looking keenly at you as the solution to all their problems was a tad overwhelming.

"Do sit, Miss Fitzgerald," Mrs Hampton had saved one of her best dining room chairs for Clara – the one with real green velvet on the seat (not this velveteen so many were choosing to buy instead!)

Clara sat and spotted Mrs Wilton at the back of the room. The woman gave her a little wave.

"Before I begin tonight," Mrs Hampton said to her guests, "I would like to introduce Miss Clara Fitzgerald, who I have especially invited to assist us with our problem. Miss Fitzgerald has assured myself and Mrs Wilton that she will be the finest example of discretion while working on our behalf. I hope we can all agree that something must be done?"

There was a chorus of 'hear, hear' from the guests, and Clara almost smiled at how formal they were all being.

"Miss Fitzgerald has asked to see any letters that you may have kept, to help her determine who is behind this. I know some of you were good enough to bring those letters tonight and I would now like to collect them in this brown envelope. I believe it would be helpful to Miss Fitzgerald if you were to note your name on the back of the letters, however, each one will be placed in this envelope privately and no one but Miss Fitzgerald will ever see their contents. Is that agreeable?"

There was another chorus of assent and the envelope was handed round. Clara was surprised to see that the majority of the audience produced a letter and inserted it in the envelope. She had fully expected that most had already been burned or destroyed in some way. Mrs Hampton collected the envelope and placed it on a small occasional table beside her.

"Now, perhaps I can hand over to Miss Fitzgerald, who would no doubt like to ask a few questions," Mrs Hampton took a step back and Clara was now centre-stage. Her stomach dropped.

Self-consciously Clara rose from her chair and faced the assembled poison pen victims.

"Well…" she stared at all their desperate faces. "I think I would like to begin by asking when the letters started to arrive? Does anyone know who received the first one?"

There was a huddled conversation among the audience, as they conferred on the subject. Finally, a pale small hand rose from the crowd, and a woman stood up. She was dressed in black and looked like a widow from a century ago. She was frail and shrank from the stares of her neighbours. In a faint voice the woman declared.

"I think I was the first."

"That is Mrs Uxbridge," Mrs Hampton informed Clara in a clear, crisp voice. Mrs Hampton was clearly used to public speaking.

"Mrs Uxbridge, when did you receive this letter?" Clara asked.

"It was the beginning of November. I think it was around Bonfire Night. I remember because I considered throwing it onto the bonfire when they burned the Guy, but then I thought it might flutter off and someone would see it," Mrs Uxbridge looked small among the assembled guests. "It was a very ghastly thing."

"Did you have any indication of who might have sent it, or why?"

"No. It came completely out of the blue."

"Thank you, Mrs Uxbridge," Clara said. "I would very much like to speak to all of you individually, to privately discuss the letters, as it may offer a clue to the culprits. Has anyone any suspicion as to who might have sent the letters?"

There was silence from the assembled guests, though Clara wasn't convinced that meant that no one suspected anything. Rather, she imagined people preferred not to voice their thoughts in public, less someone should ask them how they had reached their conclusions. Clara felt that here were a lot of people who didn't really trust one another, and who had an awful lot of secrets.

"Has no one noticed a pattern to the letters? Perhaps

they tend to arrive on a certain day, or time of the month?" she tried to nudge them a little.

"Mine arrived on a Thursday," Mrs Uxbridge said quietly.

"Mine came on a Wednesday," someone else said.

"Mine popped through the door on a Saturday. I was most relieved it came then, because Frank was at the football match and didn't see it," another voice added.

"I had one on a Saturday too…"

"All right, so they come on different days," Clara interrupted before everyone started to talk at once. "Are they hand delivered or do they come by post?"

"The post," Mrs Wilton said quickly.

"And has anyone kept the envelope for their letter?"

There was a general shaking of heads.

"Did anyone happen to notice the post mark on the envelope?" Clara asked.

"Oh yes!" a woman raised her hand from the back. "I was expecting a letter from my sister and I made a point of looking at the post mark to see if the letter was from her. It wasn't, unfortunately. The post mark was for Brighton."

"Thank you," Clara made a note in the little book she kept for such purposes. "So we must assume the culprit is local and not concerned about trying to hide their tracks."

"Is all this going to help?" there was a man sitting by the fireplace, he looked belligerent. "I want this person found and dealt with! The shock that letter gave my wife could have done her great harm!"

"And you are?"

"Mr Joshua Summerton," the man announced proudly. "General grocer. The letter my wife received was just filth, pure filth!"

"I intend to do everything in my power to find the culprit, Mr Summerton," Clara told him, wondering what secrets had been hinted at in the letter to his wife.

"Might I suggest," Mrs Hampton interjected, "that we all arrange a time for Miss Fitzgerald to speak with us individually and privately?"

"I think that might be the way forward," Clara agreed, though she was a tad annoyed at the interruption.

The next half-hour was occupied with taking the names and addresses of each person, and arranging a time when Clara could call on them. She soon had her diary brimming with appointments, and she began to wonder how she would ever find time to investigate Inspector Park-Coombs' concerns.

After arranging interviews, the guests retired to their homes. Mrs Prinner was among the last to leave and seemed reluctant, on the whole, to speak to Clara.

"Mrs Prinner, when might I call on you?" Clara pressed her.

"Well… well, it's my washing day tomorrow, and that means I will be so busy, and then on a Wednesday I do my baking, and the house gets in such a state."

"What about Thursday?"

"Oh dear, no, little Simon goes to visit his grandmother while I do my shopping in town."

"Friday?"

"That's a fish day. My husband owns a number of ships and on Fridays he brings home the best of the catch to gut and smoke at home. I couldn't possibly have someone round then."

"Saturday, perhaps?" Clara said in exasperation, she knew the woman was being deliberately evasive.

"Saturday the other children aren't at school."

"I don't mind children," Clara said calmly.

"That's not what I meant. I'll have so much to do. Clothes to mend, the boys' trouser knees are always being ripped, and I will have socks to darn and all sorts to get ready for the week ahead."

"I will take up as little of your time as possible."

"But… but my husband will be home."

"Mrs Prinner, do you not wish to talk to me about your letter?" Clara spoke louder than she meant to because she was growing cross, but it did the trick, because the remaining people in the room suddenly turned and looked at Mrs Prinner.

The woman blushed. No one else had refused an interview, in fact, they had all been only too glad to arrange a time and date. Mr Summerton's unpleasantly hard gaze fell on the unfortunate woman.

"What's this?" he demanded.

"I'm… I'm just so busy at the moment…" Mrs Prinner didn't meet his eye.

"We are all very busy Mrs Prinner. For my part, I will be closing the shop early one afternoon so I can speak with Miss Fitzgerald. I am sure you must be able to spare an hour somewhere in your busy week."

Mrs Prinner blushed even harder.

"I really don't think I can be much help," she mumbled.

"That is for Miss Fitzgerald to decide," Mr Summerton said pompously, like some High Court Judge passing sentence.

"Whatever you confide in me, I shall not repeat," Clara assured the woman, trying to remove Mr Summerton from the conversation. "I will not even say anything to your husband, should you wish."

"He has seen the letter," Mrs Prinner said without a qualm. "I have no secrets from him. That's why he knew it was all nonsense."

"Then why be afraid to speak with me?" Clara asked pointedly.

Mrs Prinner merely shook her head.

"Come on Thursday, about four o'clock. I should be home by then," she said hastily, before turning abruptly and leaving.

"Odd one that," Mr Summerton said, loud enough that the exiting Mrs Prinner was bound to hear him. "Lot of family problems."

Clara wondered what he meant, but it was the wrong time to ask. She arranged the last few interviews with the remaining guests, then she found herself alone with just Mrs Wilton and Mrs Hampton.

"Now that is settled, might I offer you some tea and cake?" Mrs Hampton said with the grace of a duchess, she looked like a woman too refined for her surroundings.

Clara acquiesced and helped Mrs Wilton clear some of the extra chairs from the room before they settled on a couch by the fire.

"A very mixed lot," Mrs Wilton said with her usual candidness. "Can't see any logic as to why they have all received letters."

"Except that they all live within a small distance of each other. I would suggest our writer is targeting a group of people he or she knows very well."

"Ah!" Mrs Wilton tapped her nose knowingly. "Good thinking, Clara, good thinking."

Mrs Hampton returned with a very pretty green glass cake stand in one hand and a tray of tea things in the other. She set both items down with casual ease; neither spilling a drop of tea or disturbing a crumb of cake. She started unstacking a pile of small cake plates and offered Clara a hearty slice of Victoria sponge. Clara felt her seams bulging at the mere sight of it.

"Now, let's get to business," Mrs Hampton sat down in a chair opposite Clara and Mrs Wilton, and folded her long legs elegantly over one another. "I kept my letter out to save time. Here it is."

Mrs Hampton felt in a pocket and took out a very neatly folded slip of paper. Clara recognised the same handwriting she had seen on Mrs Wilton's letter at once. She read the contents carefully;

Dear Mrs Hampton,

We know about your husband's drinking problem. We have seen him quite drunk and dishevelled coming home late at night. It is a disgrace. A woman such as yourself should be able to take charge of a recalcitrant husband, or are you too busy engaged in other matters? Your late night card games, for instance? Gambling is a sign of a wanton woman. We expected better of you, but you have proved yourself little more than a provincial slut raised up above herself. We hope you are suitably ashamed of your behaviour and will desist at once.

"It is all ridiculous of course," Mrs Hampton said as soon as Clara looked up from the letter. "I play Bridge with three friends on a Thursday evening. There is no gambling involved. I like the company as that is the night my husband George goes to the Conservative Club. He does not come home drunk, I might add. He has an inner ear problem that makes him giddy, it's worse at night and he tends to walk in an off-balance manner. But really, it is a genuine medical condition!"

Clara felt Mrs Hampton perhaps protested a little too heartily. Maybe Mr Hampton did have an ear problem that affected his balance, but she was also well aware that one of the draws of any club was the copious drinks they served in civilised surroundings. She wondered if Mr Hampton's ear issues were being exacerbated by a fondness for the demon drink?

"When did this arrive?"

"Over a month ago. I believe it was something like the third or fourth day of January."

"It came by post?"

"Yes."

Clara examined the letter again, not reading the words, but assessing the style of the writing.

"It looks like the same hand that wrote Mrs Wilton's letter."

"That's what I thought," Mrs Wilton said.

"Who would know about your Thursday night arrangement?" Clara enquired.

"My friends, of course, and I suppose their husbands and perhaps their servants if they have any. They may have mentioned it to other friends and I suppose anyone who lives in this road must see them come to my house."

"And would the same apply to your husband's visits to the Conservative Club?"

"Yes, and all his friends at the club know about his visits, naturally. I suppose quite a few people would know of it."

"Hmm," Clara said softly. "This 'provincial' business, what is that about?"

"I was born on a farm not far outside Hove. My father was a respectable businessman with 100 acres to his name. My brother inherited the farm and has since added another fifty acres. I suppose, technically, I am of provincial stock, but I resent the implication that I am some country lass who has risen above her station in life," Mrs Hampton huffed. "Quite frankly, it was that part of the letter that annoyed me the most."

"Well, thank you for your time ladies. I shall update you as soon as I am able." Clara carefully placed Mrs Hampton's letters with the others and rose from her seat.

"Thank you again Miss Fitzgerald. We must find this rogue at once. It is really quite despicable." Mrs Hampton followed her to the door, "I hope to see you soon."

Mrs Wilton left the house with Clara and for a while they walked together.

"Tell me, Mrs Wilton, of the people we met tonight, are any of them likely to have secrets they might fear being exposed?"

"Oh!" Mrs Wilton was genuinely startled by the question. "I suppose it is possible. I mean, everyone has secrets. If you ask me the Summertons have something to hide. They arrived here about five years ago and I have yet to hear any hint of their life before Brighton. It is quite the mystery."

Clara nodded.

"Anyone else?"

Mrs Wilton gave the question some thought.

"Mr Johnson is a very quiet soul, and I do sometimes wonder if he might have a few skeletons in the closet."

"I am seeing him on Friday, I believe," Clara replied. "Works as a salesman for an agricultural goods firm, doesn't he?"

"Yes. Travels a great deal. No wife, no sign of a family."

Clara filed this away in her memory.

"Well good night Mrs Wilton, if anything further springs to mind you know where to call on me."

"Yes, indeed. I am so glad you are on the case Clara!" Mrs Wilton gave a wave and hurried off to her home.

Clara wandered in the dark for a while thinking about what drove a person to write such ghastly letters. She doubted they were a very happy person. But if they thought they could elude Clara, well... they would soon discover they were very wrong.

Chapter Four

Clara had arranged her first interview with one of the poison pen victims for the following afternoon, so when she awoke on Tuesday morning, she decided to pay a call on former Constable Brompton at the hospital. Tommy was in the parlour as she hurried to leave.

"What was all that business with the Inspector?" he called out as she started to vanish.

"He thinks he has a corrupt policeman in his midst," Clara answered.

Tommy looked genuinely surprised.

"Anything I can do?"

Clara had started to dash off again, but then she paused.

"The library opens on Tuesday, doesn't it?"

"Yes," Tommy agreed.

"And they keep copies of the local newspaper in their archives, for reference?"

"I believe so."

"Could you go take a look at the reports of a drunk driver hitting Constable Brompton last summer? There might be something in them. Oh, and see if you can find some of those criminal psychology books you like to go on about from America. I want to know what motivates a person to write poison pen letters."

Tommy gave her a half-smile.

"As ever, you can't just be happy with one case."

Clara shrugged.

"Well, it keeps me busy," then she was dashing out the door.

Clara had not been back to the general hospital since she had worked there during the war. She had left the building for the last time in June 1918 to anticipate the return of her crippled brother, and had been very glad to leave it behind. Clara was not a natural nurse; blood made her queasy and she tended to get very upset when a patient died. Some of the more experienced (Clara referred to them as hard-hearted) nurses were very disapproving and had made her feel distinctly inadequate. Clara felt they had unfairly expected her to be as proficient and immune to suffering as themselves. It was the children that shook her most, and for a long time afterwards she had suffered from nightmares concerning infants with missing limbs or youngsters drenched in blood.

She had wondered how being back at the hospital now would affect her but, strangely, as she looked up at the gaunt building, she did not feel particularly alarmed or upset. It was as though she had stowed all that emotion away into some back corner of her mind. Now she just saw a building busily occupied with the mundane accidents and illnesses that occur to people in peacetime.

After a few enquiries, Clara was escorted into the basement of the building, where a large room was devoted to keeping track of patient records. She was introduced to the man in charge, Mr Brown, and left in his capable hands. Mr Brown was around sixty with carefully preened hair and a sergeant-major moustache. He wore a serviceable, but clearly well-used, dark brown suit and had a thick pair of glasses propped on his nose. He gave Clara a tour of the filing room with obvious pride.

The large basement area consisted of rows and rows of wooden filing cabinets, illuminated by several electric lights that had the bad habit of flickering at random moments. The staff consisted of three people; Brown, Miss Peeble and James Brompton. Miss Peeble worked largely at a black typewriter, typing up the scribbled doctors' notes that were sent down to her and sorting the correct papers into the patients' files. She was kept extremely busy and was a dab-hand at translating the cryptic scrawl doctors are renowned for using on their most important notes.

James Brompton was considered the most junior clerk in the filing room and, Mr Brown confided quietly, was likely to remain that way. His role, though relatively simple, was vital for keeping the filing room in good order. Each morning, James would come into the room and find patient files on his desk ready to be organised into the alphabetical filing system. He would take the top folder and create a label for it which would help when it came to finding it again. Once the label was glued to the folder he would check the contents of the file to ensure nothing was missing. It rarely was, Mr Brown assured Clara, for Miss Peebles was a stickler for detail and had been known to run down a doctor who had failed to fill in all the patient forms correctly. James would then place the folder into its relevant cabinet, based on the patient name. At any point during the course of the day messages would be sent down requesting a patient file and it was James' duty to retrieve the file and take it to the relevant doctor.

"In some cases, that can be quite challenging. Say, for instance, we have a number of patients with the same name, knowing which one to pick is impossible and you have to take the whole lot to the doctor to make sure you have the correct one," Mr Brown gave a sigh. "Doctors expect us to work miracles down here. They ask for a file on Mrs King, well, we have ten Mrs Kings on file at least. So you ask if they could be more specific and they say something like, 'oh she was the one with the usual case of gout'. As you can imagine, we are kept very busy."

Clara nodded, looking about the corridors of filing cabinets.

"How long do you keep patient files for?" she asked.

"Now there is a question!" Mr Brown chuckled to himself, as if Clara had stumbled on some secret joke. "We keep a patient's notes throughout their lifetime; never know when you might need them. But we originally planned on destroying the relevant notes after the patient was deceased, however, the doctors complained, said you never could tell when you might want to refer back to an old case for help on a new one. So we don't destroy any of them anymore. Our oldest files are from the 1870s when the administrator of the hospital first started record keeping."

"Impressive," Clara said, knowing a man who liked to be praised for his humble work when she saw one. "You will need more space soon."

"Oh, I dare say they will open another basement section for us," Mr Brown shrugged, untroubled by the thought. "You know, we have people come from hospitals all over the country to admire our filing system. Many hospitals still don't bother at all to keep records. I really don't know how they manage."

"Quite," Clara wondered if somewhere in this valley of files there was one marked C. Fitzgerald. "Might I speak to James now?"

"Why, of course, I have delayed you so long. He is over there, working on the morning's files," Mr Brown showed Clara to a desk in the centre of the basement where a young man was neatly filling in a small card label, half-hidden behind a stack of brown folders. "James, this is Miss Fitzgerald."

James Brompton stood and held out a hand to Clara. She shook it with a smile.

"Inspector Park-Coombs asked that I would pop in and check on you," Clara explained.

"James, why don't you go for an early tea break? Then you can chat with Miss Fitzgerald in private."

James grinned at his boss, clearly pleased with the notion of an early pause from his work at the desk.

"This way, Miss Fitzgerald," he said to Clara, easing his way around the desk, past a large filing cabinet, and leading her to a small room at the far side of the basement.

It was barely bigger than a large cupboard, but the room had been furnished with a sink and a kettle, and one rather battered kitchen chair. Behind a door at the very end, Clara glimpsed a toilet. The filing department was self-contained and need not venture upstairs for anything unless asked. James motioned her to take the chair and upturned a metal bucket for himself. He took two cups off a shelf and began to warm the kettle on a small stove ring squashed between the sink and the wall.

"Is the Inspector worried about me?" he asked, a frown crossing his rather innocent face.

"No, not at all. He just wanted me to drop by and see that you were doing all right and were happy."

"Oh yes miss, I am quite happy."

Clara took a good look at the young man before her. He was about twenty-five, tall and lanky, with fair, unruly hair that fluffed up in curls around his ears. He had bright blue eyes, which shone with a child-like delight for life, and he rarely lost the smile from his face. Clara found herself thinking of him as a five-year-old child in an adult's body. He had that innocent and wondering look one associates with the very young, but not with a grown man who was formerly a police constable. Clara was beginning to understand what the Inspector had meant about Brompton being no longer suitable for police work. His peaceful nature made her balk at having to raise the spectre of his accident before him. Fortunately, Brompton offered her an opening on the subject.

"The Inspector worries an awful lot since I had my accident," Brompton rather stiffly lowered himself onto the bucket, a slight grimace crossing his face as he bent his knees.

"Yes, he mentioned you were in an accident. Was it long ago?"

"Last summer, I think," James scratched at the curls over his left ear, ruffling them further, "The Inspector would know. Time is all rather hazy after that. I am dreadful with dates. Sometimes I get up on a Sunday morning and try to come to work, and my mother has to stop me!"

James gave an amused laugh at his own failings.

"What sort of an accident was it?" Clara asked casually.

"Oh, a road accident. Drunk driver, or so they said. They never caught him."

"What happened?"

"I was a policeman back then," James grinned. "I quite liked that too. I used to walk all over the place keeping an eye out for trouble. I had a whistle to blow if I needed help, and a truncheon. I was patrolling the lanes outside Hove. There isn't much about there, but there are a few farms. I had a torch if I needed it, but mostly I just followed my feet and watched the stars. It was very peaceful. I was walking down Beggar's Lane, I remember that well enough, which is odd considering all the other stuff I forget. I think I heard the car, but a little too late. I suppose it hit me. At least, that's what they say."

"You don't remember anything else?"

"No," the kettle behind James began to whistle and he stood to pour hot water into the teapot. His eyes alighted on the two cups standing nearby and a look of confusion spread over his face.

Clara noticed.

"You were making me a cup of tea too," she said.

"Ah, yes," James' face relaxed and his smile returned. "I wondered why there were two cups. That's the sort of problem I have all the time."

He sat down again and absently leaned back as if in the

chair Clara was occupying. Fortunately, the sink was behind him, and his shoulders came against it before he ended up on the floor.

"And after the accident James? What happened then?"

"Do you mean my road accident?" James had lost the thread of the conversation.

"Yes, I do. Did you wake up in the hospital?"

"Yes, this one," James pointed upwards with a finger to indicate the hospital above them. "My head hurt something awful and my legs. They say I was lucky to walk again. The car must have been coming at a fair lick to injure me like that, that's what the Inspector said, must have been coming at a fair lick. My head's not been right since. I forget things a lot. Mother gets upset about it, but father says she should be happy she still has a son. Lots of people don't, you know, because of the war."

Clara wondered if there was any point trying to ask James whether someone in the police force wished him harm. Would James even remember such a thing, assuming he had noticed at the time?

"Inspector Park-Coombs is still trying to find the man who knocked you down," she hedged around the topic. "Do you ever give any thought as to who it might have been?"

"No," James shrugged.

"What of your fellow constables? Do any of them visit you?"

James pulled a strange face; it was not so much confusion as anger, mingled with disgust. For a second Clara thought she had hit on something. Then he relaxed.

"No. I don't see any of them," James stood and began to pour out tea.

"I thought you might have had friends among the force," Clara tried, hoping to stir whatever memory had caused his strange expression.

"I think I used to," James said. "Sometimes I think I did, then other times I am not so sure."

"Were there people you didn't get on with then?"

James handed her a cup of tea.

"Maybe. I somehow feel there was but... I can't remember," James screwed up his face, the difficulty he was having trying to remember things for Clara was upsetting him.

Clara decided she should not press him further for the moment.

"Never mind, James. Here is my card, perhaps if you do remember anything you could contact me," She pulled out one of her business cards from her handbag and passed it to him.

"I like labels," James said, examining the card with great care. "I don't always remember names these days, but labels I can read. People send down notes with names on for me to find, I can do that because the name is written down. It's very helpful because I would just forget otherwise. Thank you, Miss Fitzgerald, I've never had a card like this before."

Clara smiled at him, such an innocent in a man's body. She wasn't sure whether to feel sorry for him or not. In some ways he was truly content, in a manner most people rarely achieved.

"I ought to be going," she drained her tea, which was quite ghastly, and placed the cup on the side. "Thank you for speaking to me James."

The lad grinned.

"Come again, if you want," he said.

Clara threaded her way through the filing cabinets and found Mr Brown by his desk at the door. He looked up with a thoughtful smile.

"Was that helpful Miss Fitzgerald?"

"In a way," Clara sighed. "I can't help thinking how cruel life is. How in just a moment a promising career can be swept away and a man changed forever."

"Yes, I suppose you could see it like that. But at least James is still with us."

"There is that."

Mr Brown offered to show her the way out of the

basement. Clara gladly accepted, not wishing to become lost in the many corridors and rooms of the hospital. Outside again she said goodbye to Mr Brown and wrapped her coat tightly around her in the February breeze. She had half an hour to spare before her first interview with a poison pen victim. She decided a brisk walk would fill the time adequately and perhaps burn off some of that cake she had eaten the night before. Clara strode out onto the pavement, her thoughts still on James Brompton.

Chapter Five

Annie negotiated the front steps of the library with Tommy's wheelchair, and deposited him in the main reading room.

"There you are. I shall be back in a couple of hours after I have done the shopping," she squeezed his hand and vanished back out the door.

Tommy glanced around the room. In-between the tall book shelves there were a series of long tables, where people could sit and browse through books or documents they had ordered from the archives. He rolled himself to the head librarian's desk and asked if he could order copies of the local newspaper from the summer of 1920. The librarian, Mr Dean, knew Tommy well and soon had the request forms filled out for him. Tommy made his way to the card catalogue to pass the time while he waited.

He was thumbing through the psychology section when someone bumped into his wheelchair.

"Dreadfully sorry!"

Tommy glanced up into the round face of a young woman. She was a bit older than him and dressed very well in tweed. Her arms were full of books, which had caused her to fail to notice his wheelchair.

"No need to worry," Tommy smiled. "Do you need a hand there?"

"I do seem to have been rather ambitious over the number of books I could carry at once."

"Dump them on me," Tommy grinned. "And then we can scuttle over to the reading table."

"Honestly? You are very kind."

The woman placed several books in Tommy's lap. He was intrigued by the titles. Several were on Brighton, but one was on poisons, and another was by a famous criminal psychologist in America. In fact, it was one of the books Tommy was looking for.

"Interesting volumes," he said as the woman rolled his chair up to one of the tables.

"Yes, I am doing a bit of research."

Tommy took a good look at this well-dressed woman with a Roman nose and bright, intelligent eyes.

"On Brighton?" he asked.

"In part. I am a writer, you see, and I had half a mind to set my next novel in Brighton. But I can't really decide. I am so much more familiar with Torquay as a coastal resort. I don't want to get anything wrong."

"No, naturally. What sort of writing?" Tommy was eyeing up the poisons book.

"Crime fiction," the woman gave him an abashed smile. "Some people find it rather vulgar."

"I don't," Tommy said quickly. "In fact, my sister is a private detective. I am here on her behalf. She has asked me to research an accident from last summer. It may have been less than accidental, if you see what I mean. As we speak, she is interviewing the victim."

"How exciting," the woman beamed with genuine interest. "Does she get much work?"

"Yes, a fair bit. It was slow at first, until people realised she was just as good as any man."

"Do you know, my first book was about a private detective," The woman smiled proudly. "I would love to meet your sister."

"I am sure that can be arranged."

"Call me Agatha," Agatha held out her hand to shake.

"Tommy," Tommy answered as he took it. "I would love to read your book."

"I shall arrange a signed copy for you. I say, there is a person approaching with a lot of newspapers."

"That would be for me," Tommy motioned at a library assistant burdened down with several issues of the Brighton Gazette from the previous summer. The assistant dropped the newspapers on the reading table with relief.

"All the issues from between June and August 1920," The assistant said, a slightly peeved look on his face. "I hope you find what you are looking for."

"Looks like you will be busy," Agatha nodded at the pile of papers.

"Well, I know what I am looking for, at least," Tommy took the top newspaper off the pile and was greeted by a large photograph of last summer's carnival. The by-line under the picture read Oliver Bankes. Tommy smiled to see the Fitzgeralds' friend's name in print. Above the picture ran the headline – "Ancient Mummy in Carnival actually Dead Crook!"

Flicking through the first few pages, Tommy found nothing but reports and opinion columns on the drama that had occurred at the carnival last August. Clara had, naturally, been involved. In fact, she had solved the case. Any other news that had happened at the time of the incident had been squeezed into the last few pages of the paper, tucked among 'Mother's Corner', assorted adverts and the sports pages. There was no mention of a policeman being knocked down by a car.

Tommy picked up the next issue, working backwards through time. Again there was a fair amount on the carnival, including a special offer run by the Gazette to get entry tickets for half price. Tommy skimmed over adverts for yearling sheep, Greaves' Digestion Pills and Pear's soap. Under a column headed 'Home News' he

spotted a small notice that gave him a clue, it read –
"News has reached the Gazette that the police constable injured in a hit and run accident in July has recovered sufficiently to be discharged from hospital and is now steadily recovering at home."

July! Tommy rapidly removed the June issues from his pile of papers and started on the first July paper. He took care to check each article, even those printed under the small 'News in Brief' section, but there was nothing about a policeman, so he took up the next issue. He had hardly turned two pages when a headline grabbed his eye – "Drunk Driver blamed for Accident, Constable in Serious Condition." Tommy read on;

"Last evening, around 11pm, Police Constable James Brompton was walking his usual route past White's farm when he was struck down by a car. The first person to the scene of the accident, Mr White, of the aforementioned farm, stated that he had heard a car engine roaring along the lane behind his farm and then a thud, followed by the car driving off. Mr White went to investigate as he has had sheep hit by speeding drivers before. He found Constable Brompton lying in the lane, his head very battered and bloody. Having no telephone, Mr White called for his son, and sent him the two miles to the Ship Inn, where the innkeeper was able to ring for assistance. An ambulance and a police car arrived within the hour, and Constable Brompton was taken to hospital. No sign of the driver who caused the collision was found, though the police advise the public to be alert to any vehicle with signs of damage to its bonnet or front end. Constable Brompton remains in a dangerous condition in hospital and there is much fear for his life."

Tommy copied the article from the paper into a notebook. He went through the next two issues of the paper, but there was no mention of anything more concerning Brompton's accident until he came to the first issue of August. It was then he spotted a letter on the correspondence page;

"Dear Sir – the matter of the police constable knocked down a few weeks ago outside White's farm remains unresolved. The car that hit him seems to have mysteriously vanished. It is my contention that there is some criminal matter involved in this, other than the obvious crime of hitting a person in a vehicle and then fleeing. How many cars are there in Brighton? Surely, if it was a local vehicle, some bright eyed neighbour would have noticed damage to it? There can only be a handful of car owners within the area, and the police might find it useful to visit them all and assess their vehicles, if they have not already done so. Equally, I know of only one garage in Brighton and Hove capable of repairing bodywork; have they been interviewed about vehicles they have recently attended to? There seems to be a greater mystery to this matter than merely who the driver behind the wheel was. I believe we are dealing with something far more alarming. I hope some reader may be able to assuage my concerns.

Yours Sincerely, Colonel A. J. Fairbanks (formerly Chief Inspector, Scotland Yard)"

Tommy copied the letter out diligently, and then looked at the correspondence pages from later issues to see if anyone had responded to Colonel Fairbanks. No one had. Who was this man from Scotland Yard? Clearly a retired Londoner, come to seek the peace of a seaside town, yet unable to quite leave police-work behind him. Was it just suspicion on his part that made him suggest there was something more to Brompton's accident than sheer bad luck? Or did he know something? Tommy realised Clara would be ecstatic with this find, this could be a whole new lead into Brompton's case.

"You see to be having more luck than me," Agatha glanced up from her own books. "I think setting a crime at the Brighton Pavilion might be a little gauche, don't you?"

Tommy grinned at her.

"Unless it happens to be about someone killing the

architect who designed the thing."

"True. True," Agatha closed her books. "I really don't know. I feel I have this idea for a great plot burrowing about at the back of my mind, but for the life of me I can't bring it into focus. I took this rather abrupt holiday to try and rankle it out. I thought some peace and quiet away from the family might help."

"It will come," Tommy said though, in truth, he knew very little about the art of writing, or the woes of writer's block. "Try not to force it."

As he spoke he spotted Annie returning with her basket of shopping.

"Ah, I shall have to be going."

Agatha looked over in the direction of Annie.

"Perhaps we shall meet again? I would really like to meet your sister. I am staying at the Grand Hotel. Call in for tea any time. They start serving at 4pm, and I make a point of being back for their delightful crumpets."

She quickly scribbled her name and room number on a slip of paper and passed it to him.

"Thank you, I shall endeavour," Tommy assured her.

Annie came around the reading table, looking at the heap of newspapers with a strange expression, as if she was itching to tidy them away into the dustbin. Annie hated untidiness, especially when it involved papers.

"Any luck?" she asked.

"I think so. We better get this back to Clara," he turned to Agatha. "Goodbye, I shall try and have Clara call on you."

"Do, do. I really could use the distraction."

Agatha gave him a little wave as he was pushed away by Annie. She picked up the volume on poisons and went back to refreshing her memory on the quantities needed to poison a full-grown man with Strychnine.

Chapter Six

Mrs Zelda Mann was like a nervous little bird. She fluttered and flittered. Her hands danced in her lap, and her eyes darted all about the room as she talked. She was around forty and politely termed herself an amateur artist, specialising in flower studies in oils. There was one of her paintings on the wall above the fire; a brash canvas of reds, yellows and greens portraying a much larger than life, and slightly abstract, primrose. She liked to call her paintings 'modern', but admitted to herself that many professional artists would consider them rather twee, or worse, that she was trying too hard. Zelda had no confidence in herself.

She had married at eighteen, her husband was seven years her senior, and even at the time of their marriage he was regarded as a remarkable chemist. He now worked in London during the week, at a large pharmaceutical company, creating all manner of new and exciting products.

"He is largely involved in experiments concerning synthetic materials," she told Clara over a cup of tea. "He believes it may be possible to invent a completely new material that will replace for good such things as cotton or silk. Imagine the possibilities!"

Zelda was proud of her husband and it showed as she talked. She had read his papers diligently and, despite her own self-deprecations, she was really a very intelligent woman who understood many of the chemical equations involved in her husband's work.

"He brings samples home sometimes. Very tiny amounts at the moment. But he shows me them. If they can only discover the right formula it will be really revolutionary. My husband believes synthetics would be so cheap to manufacture that, in the future, no one need be without clothes or shoes. Imagine a world where even the poorest was well-dressed and free from the torments of cold weather and sickness!"

Clara nodded, the vision was certainly nice. Clara was more of a cynic, however. She didn't believe anything in life was ever free. Someone would attempt to make money from this world-saving product somewhere along the line. Clara nudged the subject back onto Zelda's paintings. She had read the hate letter sent to the woman and knew it was her art that had aroused the writer's ire.

"I try to capture the spirit of the flower," Zelda said softly, her hands miming the action of a flower opening in her lap. "Anyone can paint a begonia, but what of the essence of that plant? What of the way it makes you feel as you stare at the petals, or its scent, or how it can sum up a whole glorious summer in one glance? That is what I try to capture, though, I confess, I fail more often than I succeed."

"How long have you been painting?"

"Since the children were old enough to hardly need me," Zelda gave a sad half laugh. "They drift away as they grow up. Especially sons. I have been luckier than most mothers. Both my boys came through the war unscathed. Now Michael is at university studying biology, and Peter is spending a year in Argentina, on a scientific expedition investigating the way air currents affect mechanical flight. They are very bright lads and very ambitious. Peter is very good at gliding. It is not as popular over here as in Europe and, to my horror, he actually chose to go to Germany for a year to learn. But he wants to work in aviation and says gliding is the way to understand how planes cut through the air. He is just nineteen, but he has been more places than I have ever been in my life."

"I imagine you miss your sons a lot."

"Yes. The house is very quiet. I have a cat, but cats are rather difficult company. Mainly I paint."

"Has your work ever been exhibited?"

"Last year," Zelda suddenly beamed with a rare moment of pride. "I booked the Methodist hall for a whole week. They were very accommodating, seeing as my pictures were nothing racy or offensive. Flowers rarely inflame the passions, do you not find?"

"Indeed."

"It was rather a success. I sold three pictures, and Mr Spranks at the stationers asked if he could use one of my designs on a greetings card. I was elated and spent a number of hours in his office working out the details, before having the picture miniaturised and turned into a print. They have a special way of printing colour greetings cards, it was quite fascinating. Mr Spranks was delighted with the result and has sold over a dozen already. He has talked about printing more as postcards for the summer tourist season."

"That sounds very exciting," Clara said. "But I assume it was this time spent with Mr Spranks that sparked the letter you received?"

"Yes," Zelda suddenly lost all her animation, her hands went flat in her lap. "It was just after I received the first sample cards. I was so delighted with them, and took them at once to show my sister who lives two streets away. When I came back, I noticed the envelope on the doormat. It was addressed to me, but I didn't recognise the writing. Oh, I still wish I had never opened the horrid thing."

Zelda put her head in her hands for a moment. Then she composed herself.

"You have read it. You know it implied that I had been having an illicit affair with Mr Spranks and that he only turned my painting into a card because we were... intimate."

"It's a nasty thing to say."

"Yes. Bad enough how it impinged on my honour and reputation, but it made me feel as if no one believed my work good enough to merit such attention on its own. I felt quite sick about it."

"You mustn't imagine the feelings or opinions of the letter writer are representative of the thoughts of everyone else," Clara reassured her. "People gossip, no doubt, but anyone can see your work merits attention for its creative force alone."

Both women glanced up at the over-sized primrose on the wall. Clara had quoted a line out of a recent magazine article on modern artists she had read to comfort Zelda, but she hadn't been entirely lying. Zelda's work was a little naïve, but it was bright, cheerful and full of character. Just the sort of thing that would sell well on a postcard, to tourists full of holiday spirit. A satisfied smile slowly crept over Zelda's face.

"A vicar bought one of my paintings, you know," Her hands jittered in her lap, telling their own story independent of her words. "He said it would brighten up the rectory and make a change from hunting scenes. He picked one which portrayed a Lily of the Valley, for the spiritual metaphor."

"I truly believe these letters are sparked by jealousy, Mrs Mann. The person who wrote this, saw your success and was envious."

Zelda cocked her head on one side like a little bird as she contemplated this suggestion.

"Then I shall not let it worry me further."

"Don't. Now, have you had any thoughts about who might have sent the letter?"

"I didn't recognise the handwriting," Zelda said apologetically. "Which at least means it is not one of my regular correspondents."

"Have any of your neighbours or acquaintances appeared disregarding of your success?"

"No, not that I can think of. I don't boast about it, you see. I did deliver a lot of invitations to the exhibition. That seemed prudent."

"How many?"

Zelda did a quick calculation in her head.

"Yes, I had 200 printed up. It was extravagant, I know, but I was dreading no one would come. I gave one to all my friends and sent some to the notables of Brighton, like the Mayor – he came by the way, quite a surprise! – And then the rest I posted through the doors of the houses in this road and the next three. I suppose anybody who received an invitation could have been the letter writer."

"Two hundred suspects already, not to mention those who saw the exhibition notice in the paper, or heard about it from friends."

Zelda looked disheartened.

"However," Clara corrected herself, "what I would say, is that the person behind the writing had to know about your talks with Mr Spranks. That must narrow the field."

"Yes," Zelda nodded enthusiastically.

Clara wondered if there was any way of determining exactly who knew of Zelda's talks with the stationer. Probably not. Brighton was a relatively small town and people talked. There would be the staff at Mr Spranks' shop for a start. They would know of Zelda's visits, not to mention Zelda's friends and anyone they had mentioned it to. And who knew how many people Mr Spranks had told? After all, he would want to publicise his new venture. And then, when the cards came out, the arrangement would be extremely public. No, once more the suspect list was expanding rather than contracting.

"Thank you for your time Mrs Mann," Clara stood. "I am off to see the Livingstones next."

"Oh, a lovely couple!" Zelda clapped her hands. "Even considering…"

She bit her lip. Clara waited for an explanation.

"Well," Zelda was glancing around again, as if the furniture or wallpaper might save her from the blunder. "Well, Mr Livingstone's father, as I hear it, was a businessman with interests abroad. He married a Caribbean woman!"

"Is that a problem?" Clara asked innocently.

"Not to me!" Zelda said quickly. "I am an enlightened woman. I vote, you know! But some people resent Mr Livingstone being so, ahem, coffee-coloured."

"I'll bear that in mind," Clara said, imagining it was Mr Livingstone's hue that had been targeted in the letter to him. She had only met Mrs Livingstone at Mrs Hampton's gathering, and the woman had apologised for no longer having the poison pen letter she was sent. Her husband had burned it.

Clara said her goodbyes to Zelda Mann, a promise being extracted from her, as she left, that she would, most assuredly, attend Zelda's next exhibition. Clara walked down the road four houses to the home of Mr and Mrs Livingstone and rang the doorbell. Mrs Livingstone answered the door dressed rather smartly for an afternoon at home; she was even wearing a string of pearls. Clara guessed she had dressed up for the interview.

Clara was shown to the back parlour where Mr Livingstone was pacing back and forth in a grey pin-stripe suit. He turned as Clara entered. Mr Livingstone hesitated a moment, then offered his hand to shake.

"Thank you for coming, Miss Fitzgerald," he said in the King's English.

"I hope I have not caused you any inconvenience," Clara indicated Mr Livingstone's suit.

"Oh, no bother. I was due a day off. Lily will tell you I work too hard."

"That he does," Mrs Livingstone came into the room behind Clara and smiled at her husband.

"What sort of business are you in?" Clara asked

curiously as she was offered a chair.

"Imports, mainly. Chocolate, coffee, sugar. All the glories of the East Indies," Mr Livingstone rolled his eyes and made a motion to the colour of his skin. "We do quite well. Father thinks I am 'slumming it' having this quaint terrace in Brighton."

"But it is most delightful," Mrs Livingstone interrupted. "I couldn't stand having a huge house to run. All those empty rooms! Ghastly! This is perfect."

Mr Livingstone gave the shrug of a spouse who knows when to lose a battle.

"I suppose we ought to get down to business," Mr Livingstone sank into a chair. His wife offered tea to Clara, but she declined, having drunk two cups already with Zelda.

"Let's begin with the basic details. When did you receive the letter, if you can recall?" Clara asked.

"Oh, I can recall," Mrs Livingstone's previously light and happy tone suddenly became hard and bitter. Her smile faded and her face seemed to lose its softness, to be replaced by a grey hardness. "It was the 3rd of October. Charlie was at work as usual in London," She motioned to her husband. "I had been working through the household bills when the post came. The maid brought a bundle of letters to me, mostly the usual thing. There was only one which was written in a hand I didn't recognise. I put it to one side and went through the important letters first. I almost forgot about it, in fact. It wasn't until the evening, around the time I expect Charlie home, that I remembered it and became curious.

"Dinner was just being put on the table when I sat down to read it. It was an obnoxious catalogue of insults and lies! I had only just finished it when Charlie came in and saw my face. I must have looked ghastly, I felt awful, like someone had struck me. Without a word I gave him the letter and he read it. He was furious. He took the letter and threw it straight into the fire."

Mr Livingstone was nodding along with his wife's

story.

"I suppose I should have kept it, but I saw the look on my wife's face and I just wanted to destroy the hurtful thing," Charlie Livingstone sighed. "It's not the first time I have been sent such things. I have learned to grow impervious to the insults people fling at someone because they are the wrong colour. I went to a boys' school where everyone was whiter than white. I endured all the usual slings and arrows schoolboys throw at someone who is different. But, to see how it affected my wife! That upset me more than the words themselves."

"I was angry, so, so angry," Mrs Livingstone added. "I was just so furious that someone would dare to say those things. Had they been in the room at the time, I swear I would have slapped them!"

Lily Livingstone was a fighter and she now radiated righteous indignation. Clara was confident that, should she find the culprit behind the letters, Lily Livingstone would make them wish they had never learned to write.

"I don't need to know the contents of the letter," Clara told them. "Unless you think it might offer some clue as to who was behind it?"

"The insults were fairly standard," Mr Livingstone shook his head. "They did not require any insider knowledge, if that is what you mean. It largely referred to marrying monkeys and people returning to the jungle they came from."

"Deeply unpleasant," Clara concurred, understanding fully why Mrs Livingstone was so furious. She would have felt the same. "Can you think of anything that happened before the letter arrived that might have triggered the writer to compose such a thing? Some of the letters seem to be responses to the person involved having a success of some kind, or something new happening in their lives?"

The Livingstones glanced at one another.

"I can't think of anything," Lily said. "Everything was ordinary."

"Father had just secured a deal to supply Fry's with cocoa beans, but no one in Brighton knew of it," Charlie added.

"It was just a thought," Clara said. "And you can't think of anyone who might have sent the letter?"

The Livingstones could not. Clara brought the interview to a close, promised to keep them informed of developments and then went back out into the road. It was drawing close to four o'clock and she had no more appointments for the day. Clara decided to head home and mull over what she had learned so far. As she was walking along, she heard the clack of a woman's shoes behind her, and suddenly Mrs Wilton was at her side.

"Well, Clara?"

Mrs Wilton had a way of inserting herself into a case as if she was Clara's assistant or, worse, a fellow private detective.

"I have hardly begun," Clara answered.

"Who have you spoken to?" Mrs Wilton probed. "That was the Livingstones' house, so clearly you have met them. Nice couple. Mr Livingstone can make a cup of coffee you would die for. He insists on putting cream in it, would you believe? The first time I tried it I was quite sceptical, but it really was delightful. Much better than milk."

Clara let Mrs Wilton ramble on; it was easier than having to answer her questions.

"So what did you learn from them?" Mrs Wilton pressed.

"All my interviews are conducted in complete confidence," Clara told her firmly.

"Naturally. But do you have any suspects in mind yet?"

Clara had to admit she didn't.

"So far the information contained in the letters is neither very secret or of a nature that implies someone who knew the victims extremely well. I fear our poison pen is a mere gossip, who picks up random stories circulating the neighbourhood, and then regurgitates them in nasty letters."

"Oh dear, that isn't helpful," Mrs Wilton was puffing slightly as she tried to keep up with Clara's brisk pace. "It could be anyone then?"

"Yes."

"Is there anything these letters can tell us about them?"

"Well, they are a person who is bitter and spiteful," Clara said, "They probably like hearing bad things about people because it makes them feel better about their own lives. I imagine they feel they have not achieved what they should have in life. Perhaps they feel the world has been unkind to them. The sort of person who puts someone else down because they feel inadequate in themselves."

"Oh dear, I know several people who fit that description," Mrs Wilton tutted to herself. "Is there nothing else?"

Clara considered, then a thought struck her.

"Some of the terms and phrases in the letters seem rather old-fashioned. The sort of thing a person of my grandmother's generation would use. That could mean we are dealing with an elderly person."

Again Mrs Wilton shrugged and sighed.

"The world is full of elderly people."

"Yes, but only a handful are cruel enough to want to deliberately hurt others."

"I shall keep my ears open for information!" Mrs Wilton assured her stoutly.

They parted at the turning in the road and Clara headed for home. She was starting to feel alarmed at the anonymity a person could maintain when writing such venomous letters. How was she to trace this person and stop them? Without more clues as to their identity, they were free to carry on tormenting the residents of Brighton. But then again, perhaps Mrs Prinner could offer the solution? If Mrs Wilton was right, that woman knew a lot more than she was letting on. Unfortunately that meeting was for another day and for the time being Clara had a number of other people to talk to. Perhaps there was some clue she had yet to see. Perhaps the letter writer had slipped up somehow? She just had to hope their success would make them careless. Now, what were the odds of that?

Chapter Seven

"Alfie Ling!" Annie slammed a bowl of boiled potatoes down on the dining room table.

Clara always thought Annie would make a good avenging angel; she was a small woman, the sort most people overlooked, but she had a good heart and an iron-will, and she could smell trouble a mile off. She had had a look of deep thought on her face ever since she had learned that Clara was looking for a corrupt policeman. It had made her small lips purse into a wasp-sting of red.

"Alfie Ling?" Clara asked cautiously, she recognised the name.

"Look no further than him for your dodgy bobby," Annie told Clara firmly. "Trouble since the day he was born, that one."

"I believe I met him last year during my investigations into the death of Mrs Greengage," Clara helped herself to potatoes.

"You did indeed. How he ever made it into the police force Heaven only knows!" Annie was bristling, her neat hands agitating over the carrots she was trying to serve. "That boy never had no good in him. He was a thief and a thug from the day he could crawl. He stole my mother's washing line once! Hung it in his own backyard and claimed his own wastrel mother had bought it! As if she ever cared about washing. The line still had my father's shirt on it!"

Annie bustled off for the gravy boat, puttering to herself.

"I think she has a grudge against Alfie Ling," Tommy said quietly across the dinner table.

"She could have a point though," Clara responded. "Does a man go from a childhood of petty crime to a lifetime of upholding the law?"

Annie returned with the gravy.

"And another thing, Ethel, who as works for the Wilkinsons at number 12, swears on her life she saw Alfie Ling having tea and cake with Mavis Palmer. And we all know what she does for a living. Now, what's a policeman doing with the likes of her?"

"You have a point Annie, but a man's past is just that, in the past."

"Hmph!" Annie snorted indignantly, before taking her place at the table.

It had taken Clara weeks to persuade Annie to eat dinner with them at the table. She decided she didn't want to ruin that by pushing her point too hard.

"However, it would be worthwhile discovering how Alfie made it into the police force. Clearly someone ignored his past record, if they checked at all," Clara said to mollify her. "As suspects go, he is certainly the obvious choice."

"What about interviewing that colonel I mentioned?" Tommy piped up. "He seemed to have some serious suspicions."

"I'll need to track him down first. The paper didn't give an address."

"I can do that," Tommy said confidently, "while you talk with Farmer White."

"Lord, it's a long journey to his farm," Clara gave a groan. "Perhaps I can borrow a bicycle?"

They had just begun to discuss the logistics of

travelling to Mr White's farm when the doorbell rang.

"Goodness! Who calls during dinner time?" Annie complained as she got up to answer it.

"White is the nearest you have to an eyewitness," Tommy continued to say as Annie left the room. "Perhaps he saw or heard more than he shared with the paper?"

"Yes. It is such a shame that Brompton's mind is so damaged. If only he could tell me what he had stumbled upon that made him a target!" Clara thought of that poor young man in the hospital, he was happy in his own way, but his life had been radically altered by one act of violence. "But, I suppose if he could, he would still be in danger from those who wished to silence him."

At that moment Annie returned.

"It's Oliver Bankes."

Clara stood from the table at once and smiled at the unexpected arrival. Oliver had visited her nearly every day while she was recuperating from her illness; their friendship had grown over pear drops and local gossip. Oliver had made a point of keeping Clara well informed about the activities of Brighton, knowing she would be going insane without being able to venture out and discover what was going on for herself. Any good private detective has to have a fine ear for rumours, innuendoes and gossip. Oliver had been Clara's supplier for all the while she was unable to get out of bed. She was pleased to see him now, they had not spoken since Sunday, and she had to admit she missed their afternoon chats. But as she smiled at Oliver, she saw the look of dismay on his face.

"I can't stay long," Oliver said apologetically. "Dad's in quite a state, I don't like to leave him alone for the moment. He received this, this morning."

Oliver dropped a letter onto the table. Clara recognised the handwriting at once. She opened the envelope and read the contents.

Dear Mr Bankes,

You are a dirty old man! We see the girls coming to your house and we know just the sort of pictures your kind take of women. You are nothing but a piece of filth and a disgrace to the neighbourhood. It would be better for everyone if you were to leave and take your disgusting habits elsewhere. If you do not go at once, we shall be forced to report your activities to the police. Not that you deserve any mercy. It is men like you who are ruining the young women of today and, we are agreed, you should be hanged for your crimes! We expect you to leave shortly and take your shame elsewhere.

"Oh dear," Clara put the letter on the table. "It's one of the nastier ones I have read."

"It upset father a great deal, I thought his heart was going to stop," Oliver shook his head sadly. "I know he is a bit of a rogue, but he wouldn't…"

Oliver paused, looking morose.

"He is very worried, which makes me wonder if there is a grain of truth to this story."

"Tell him not to fret," Clara instructed firmly. "The writer of this letter is not going to go to the police, else they risk exposing themselves too. It is an empty threat, though upsetting nonetheless."

Clara thought about where Oliver's father lived, she had been to the house once or twice before. It happened to be around the area where the other victims lived, and the wording of the note – a disgrace to the neighbourhood – suggested to Clara that the writer lived there too.

"I said I had to bring this to you at once," Oliver said. "He was in rather a state and I had to persuade him not to burn it, but in the end I think he understood. I best get back to him, he was white as a sheet when I left."

"Take care Oliver, if there is anything you need you know where we are," Clara said goodbye as Oliver hurried off, then she returned to the table and picked up the letter again.

"Have you noticed," Tommy leaned over the table, "how the letter writer always uses the term 'we' when describing themselves."

"Yes. I thought maybe it was affected, like the Royal

'we'."

"Or it could be simpler than that. Maybe there isn't just one writer?"

"The letters are all written in the same hand, I double-checked that."

"But, perhaps there is more than one person composing the material?"

Clara stared at the letter.

"A couple, perhaps? One writing the letter, the other suggesting the content?" She grimaced. "Two people so warped as to invent this rubbish."

"Do you think any of it is true?" Annie was standing at the end of the table looking worried. "I mean, the stuff about Mr Bankes?"

Clara started to say 'no', then she recalled the unfortunate incident last summer when Mr Bankes had been caught red-handed taking some indiscreet photographs at the fairground.

"That's what I thought," Annie said, catching the look that crossed Clara's face. "I don't like to say this because I think Oliver is a really nice man, but, Clara, should you be associating with someone who has such a father as that?"

"Annie!" it was Tommy who reacted before Clara did. "Oliver is a good fellow and can't help what his father does or doesn't do!"

"Well, no…" Annie admitted.

"Oliver is a dear friend," Clara added. "I shan't abandon him because of a silly letter."

Annie was silent a moment, but her lips were pursed.

"I was just thinking of your reputation," she said softly.

"You sound like the poison pen!" Tommy responded gruffly, he rarely argued with Annie, but on this occasion he was riled by her words.

"I shall worry about my own reputation," Clara said firmly, but nicely, endeavouring to be the peace-maker of the three. "I have no intention of abandoning Oliver because his father is a tad eccentric. After all, some might say that by being friends with me, he is damaging his own reputation."

"That's different!" Annie interjected sharply.

"Is it? Many would say I am an unnatural woman for running a business and investigating crimes. I would hate to think of people I call friends distancing themselves from me because of my choice of career. I would expect better than that from people I considered friends," Clara gave Annie a very pointed look and the whole matter was very rapidly dropped.

"I'll get the bread and butter pudding," Annie said quickly, turning away in a fluster.

"I can't believe…" Tommy began as she vanished down the hall.

"She is just being protective," Clara reassured him. "Think no more on it."

Tommy met her eyes slowly.

"Oliver's father isn't, ahem, dangerous… is he?"

"I doubt it," Clara said stoutly. "Now who is questioning my judgement?"

"I just want to be sure you are safe."

"And I am," Clara smiled. "Really, a woman almost coughs her last due to a bout of influenza and everyone thinks she is as dainty as a glass flower!"

"Old girl, you are the only family I've got left," Tommy pulled a sad face. "Can't have you dying on me."

"Same applies to you," Clara reached out for his hand. "Same applies to you."

Chapter Eight

Clara couldn't find a bicycle to borrow the next morning, so she set out on foot for White's farm. Along the way she managed to beg a ride from a man driving a cart full of winter fodder. He knew White's farm and was good enough to drop her near the farmyard. It was a cold, crisp day. A slight mist hung over the fields, and there were still patches of frost and ice along the roads. Clara pulled her coat around her tighter and wedged her hat on her head firmly. She wondered how all those girls who had had their hair cut outrageously short managed to keep their ears warm in this weather.

White's farm was reasonably successful and looked well maintained as Clara entered the yard. The war had been kind to Mr White. He had been subsidised by the government to turn more of his land over to arable food production, and had even managed to acquire a few more acres in the process. Clara recalled Mrs Hampton's remarks on her brother and his successful expansion of the family farm. It looked as though Mr White was enjoying similar success. Of course, whether that would continue now Britain was able to import goods safely again, was another matter.

Clara walked past a large plough, clearly in the

process of being repaired, and knocked at the farmhouse door. There was a long silence and Clara wondered if Mr White was still out in the fields. She glanced at her wristwatch (a decadent Christmas present from Tommy) and noted it was growing close to ten o'clock. Perhaps the farmer was out working?

Almost as she thought about turning around to explore the buildings about the farm, the door opened and a small, round woman, with a face like uncooked dumpling dough, peered at her.

"Good morning," Clara said. "I was hoping to speak to Mr White? I am looking into the matter of an accident that occurred behind your farm last year?"

The woman blinked at her rapidly.

"Accident?"

"The one involving Police Constable Brompton? I am looking into the matter on behalf of the family," Clara braced herself for a lie. "The police offer certain forms of compensation and the family believe their son may be due some money, as he was injured in the line of duty. But they need a few details confirmed first. I believe Mr White was first on the scene of the accident?"

"Yes, my husband was," Mrs White still looked anxious. "I just cooked his breakfast. He has been up since five, had a problem with the sheep. He got back in only ten minutes ago, or thereabouts."

As she spoke she moved back and allowed Clara into the house. The Whites' farmhouse was extremely old, with low ceilings and timber beams stretching across the uneven plasterwork. A large, plain grandfather clock ticked down time in the corner. When Mrs White closed the front door, the hall became extremely dark. There were no lights on in the house at all, despite the dull winter morning.

"This way," Mrs White gave Clara another strange look and then led her through to the kitchen.

Farmer White was sitting at a well-scrubbed kitchen table, hunched over a plate of sausages, bacon and eggs. A big farm dog lay at his feet, snoring to itself, as it absorbed heat from the nearby kitchen range. Mr White had been a farmer all his life and he was now nearly sixty. In all that time he had kept to a very rigid routine. He rose early and tended the animals, then he came home and ate a good breakfast (always three sausages, two eggs, four slices of bacon and several rounds of bread and butter) before beginning the various chores he had set himself for the day. At lunchtime he had cheese and bread, washed down with cider, then he worked on until the light began to fade, (or in summer, when his stomach began to rumble) and returned home to a hearty dinner, before sitting before the fire for an hour or two smoking a pipe and then up to bed, ready to start again the next day. Few things disrupted this routine, the war had been one of them, and now Clara arriving on his doorstep was another. Mr White stared at his breakfast, having this feeling at the back of his mind that eating in front of a visitor was somehow rude, yet also knowing his bacon would be cold soon. He was torn between carrying on as normal or dealing with this very unusual interruption. Clara decided to solve the riddle for him.

"Carry on with your breakfast Mr White, I know you are a busy man with lots to do."

Mr White gave a grunt of thanks, then started on his sausages. The farm dog at his feet gave a contented snuffle and rolled over.

"I've come to ask about the accident that occurred behind your farm last summer. The one involving the policeman?" Clara accepted a cup of tea and some bread and butter offered her by the anxious Mrs White. Much like her husband, Mrs White wasn't used to unexpected visitors. "If you could tell me everything you remember about that night it would be most helpful."

Mr White swabbed his plate with a thick slice of bread and managed to consume it in two bites. He dropped his fork and knife on the plate and leaned back with a sigh of satisfaction. When he looked up at Clara his smile was welcoming, if a little reticent.

"That was a nasty bit of business."

"Yes," Clara could only concur.

"How is the young lad?" Mrs White asked suddenly. "I think of his mother sometimes, how she must have been sick with worry. We have a son and I worry about him so."

Clara recognised Mrs White as one of the world's natural worriers, her anxiety on the doorstep had not been due to anything suspicious, as Clara had initially wondered, but a normal response from a woman who saw trouble everywhere.

"PC Brompton is quite recovered. He works at the hospital now. Sadly, his injuries prevent him from being a policeman any longer."

"How sad," Mrs White looked genuinely disheartened by the news.

"Nasty bit of business," Mr White repeated quietly.

For a time no one said anything. Clara broke the silence.

"What first alerted you to the accident?" she asked Mr White.

The farmer gave another grunt, it seemed his habit, and scratched at his thick, curling hair.

"I suppose it was the car," he said at last. "We don't get many cars hereabouts, the lane is pretty narrow and it is just dirt, not that fancy tarmacadam stuff. Hearing a car roaring along that lane got my attention, no one in their right mind would drive fast down there. You could hit anything. Back when my father was alive, there was a very unpleasant accident in that lane when some young fellow drove his car too fast around the corner. The young lady with him lost her head. We found it in the hedge."

Mr White fell silent again, his mind returning to another night twenty years ago when he had heard a terrible squeal followed by a crash, and had raced out with his father to see what had occurred. He had never desired to own a car after that gruesome scene. The driver was bad enough, a mangled mess of bones and flesh, but the woman… there had been her body, all neat in her best dress, but everything above the neck was missing. The interceding years had faded the image in his memory; he was, after all, a man who spent time around animal carcasses. Then there had come that terrible roaring engine last summer, and all in an instant the nightmares about that horrid accident two decades before came flooding back.

"I said to my wife 'damn fool driving that fast down a lane'."

"He did," Mrs White nodded eagerly. "I said I was just very glad our John had no interest in cars."

"What happened next?" Clara asked.

"It was one of those things. You couldn't help but listen. I didn't want to, in case the worst happened, but somehow I couldn't stop. I heard the car take the corner down the bottom of my field," Mr White pointed to the far side of the kitchen, indicating where, should they be able to see through the wall, his field ended. "He took that all right, though I cringed as I heard him brake. Then he was roaring up this long stretch at the back. You could hear he was going faster and faster. Then there was a cry and a terrible thudding sound, but the car just carried on. Never stopped."

"You didn't hear him even attempt to brake?"

Mr White shook his head.

"Sure as sure I was that something had been hit. I have sheep out and it crossed my mind one had stumbled into the lane and he had hit it. I grabbed up the big storm lantern and ran outside, shouting to my wife to rouse John from his bed and send him out too. I ran across the big field, I am not ashamed to say there was bile in the back of my throat. I was dreading what I might find. The car had vanished, but when I jumped over the hedge there was the lad lying in the road. He looked dead. His legs were smashed. I could see bone through his uniform. His head was in a pool of blood. I thought to myself, this boy has had it. Then I crouched down to look at his badge and found out who he were, and suddenly he gives this gurgle. Sort of a groan, I suppose, and just then John appears and I send him running to the nearest telephone to get a message to the police."

"Had you met Constable Brompton before?"

"No. I knew the police sometimes sent a man to walk the lane, but most times when it is dark I am indoors or in the middle of a field tending a sick animal. There isn't much time for talking to folk."

"And, have you ever heard this car since?"

"Never," Mr White said stoutly. "If I had I would have gone out and had a word with the driver. I imagine he scared himself with that incident. Ghastly that he didn't stop though. The doctor who came out said if we had not sent for him as quickly as we did, the lad would have been done for."

Clara imagined that was what the driver of the car had hoped.

"Thank you for your time Mr White, and for the bread and tea Mrs White. I shan't impose on you any longer."

Mrs White escorted Clara to the door. Just in the hall she paused and went to a small ornamental bowl she kept on a side table.

"I kept this silly thing," she picked up something shiny in her hand. "I don't know what it is, but I found it in the road. I suppose, I always thought it might be important."

She pressed the object, which was a piece of chromed metal, into Clara's hand. It had a shape to it, somewhat like the edge of a bird's wing. It might have come off a car, Clara supposed. Clara thanked her again and then went on her way. She glanced up and down the road outside the farm in the vain hope there might be another cart coming along that could take her back to Brighton. Failing that, she set out on foot. At least, she consoled herself, the exercise would do wonders for her waistline.

Chapter Nine

Tommy was in the Post Office looking up an address for Colonel Fairbanks, when he bumped into Agatha the writer again. She was posting several letters and looked rather in a hurry, but she stopped to talk nonetheless.

"How does the investigation go?"

"Oh, it's just the start and things are always slow at the start," Tommy replied. "How goes your research?"

"Dreadful! I am at a dead end. Brighton has just not been as inspiring as I had hoped."

"That's a shame."

"Look, Tommy, come have a pot of tea and a chat with me. I could do with someone to bounce ideas off, if you wouldn't mind."

Tommy said he didn't. He left a message for Annie with the postmistress, letting her know where he had gone. Then Agatha pushed him to the nearest tea shop and ordered a plate of small cakes and a large pot of tea.

"The problem is," she began as soon as they were settled, "getting the character of the detective just right. They have to be believable and people have to like them, or the readers simply won't care if they solve the crime or not. And it would be even worse if they hated the detective so much they actually wanted the criminal to get away with the crime!"

"Yes, I could see that being a problem," Tommy smiled.

"And then there is the dilemma of how you deal with your detective's relationship with the police. Unless he is a policeman himself, he is going to be unwelcome to the officials. Worse if you make him a woman! Gosh, imagine what the police would make of a little old lady interfering in crimes! Oh, heavens, and what if she solved the case before them! They would be appalled."

"Clara has managed to develop a working relationship with our local Inspector. Though, perhaps that is as much due to him being a very forward-thinking man. She tries not to tread on too many toes."

"That is just it! How to ensure they work together and not against each other. And it has to be believable!" Agatha sighed. "My husband thinks I fret too much over my writing."

"Nonsense," Tommy assured her. "You merely want to write the best story possible. All good artists fret over their work."

The doorbell of the teashop rang, as it had done a half-dozen times since Agatha and Tommy had sat down, but this time Tommy found himself looking up, and he saw Annie in the doorway. She looked displeased. Her eyes went to Agatha sitting in her neat dress and jacket, eating her cake in very refined, small bites. Annie was not a naturally jealous woman, but she didn't like the way Tommy had been absorbed so immediately into the aura around this writer. They could talk about crime in a way Annie never could. She grimaced at suggestions of poisonings or shootings, far too grim for polite conversation in her mind. Yet, here was Tommy eagerly discussing just those matters with this new, handsome woman – in a teashop! They were eating cake and chatting like old friends and all she had was a message slipped to her by the postmistress!

Annie didn't usually feel like a servant around

Tommy. They were friends and, if not quite equals, that was only because Annie tried to keep a certain detachment. Yet, suddenly, here she was feeling like little more than a… a… a maid!

Annie stormed into the teashop and straight up to the table. She was trying to hold in her outrage, but suspected it showed on her face.

"Annie this is Agatha, a writer," Tommy introduced them, not noticing the strange tension in the girl.

"Morning," Annie said as politely as she could to the usurper.

Agatha smiled politely back.

"Do you work for the Fitzgeralds?" she asked without meaning anything by the comment.

Annie, however, perceived it as an insult. Had Tommy not interceded she would have said something regrettable.

"Annie is a friend, a very dear friend," Tommy smiled. "She may do the housework, but it would be unfair on her to imagine her role is that of a mere servant. Isn't that right, old girl?"

Tommy's light-humoured grin flashed up at Annie and she felt her anger disintegrating. It was hard to stay angry when Tommy threw his charm on a person. She felt her righteous indignation eluding her and with it evaporated her confidence. Annie was not good around people she perceived as her social betters. They made her nervous. Her anger had temporarily overridden her unease. Now it returned as she anxiously wished to flee the teashop as fast as she could. Instead she heard Tommy inviting her to sit down and join them. Annie's stomach flipped unpleasantly. She glanced at Agatha who looked very smart in her mink stole and new season hat. Annie fingered the buttons on her own well-worn woollen coat. Yet her mouth had dried up on excuses.

"Agatha is trying to find inspiration for her new novel," Tommy explained. "Do sit down Annie and have some cake."

Annie obeyed, trying not to meet Agatha's eye.

"Annie can be quite a good detective in her own right," Tommy added.

Annie felt this was going too far.

"I only help when asked too. Crime is for the police to solve," she said, a little more sharply than she intended. "Clara gets herself into all manner of mischief."

"You don't think she performs a valuable service as a private detective?" Agatha asked her directly.

Annie was stumped. She felt her speech elude her. She wanted to run away as fast as she could. Instead she coloured and somehow mumbled.

"I suppose."

"I really must meet your sister Tommy," Agatha said. "She sounds really quite incredible."

"I think that might be over-stating her achievements," Tommy responded modestly. "But I see no reason not to introduce you. She is usually home for teatime. What have we got tonight Annie?"

Annie felt flustered as attention focused back on her. She blinked rapidly.

"Cucumber sandwiches," she said without thinking.

"Heavens, where have you found cucumbers at this time of year?" Agatha enquired.

Annie wanted to kick herself.

"No, no, I meant cold meat sandwiches," she said hastily. "And some homemade pickles."

"Annie's pickles are to die for," Tommy said enthusiastically. "Would you care to join us?"

"It would make a change from crumpets, so yes, I would."

"Excellent! Now, let's see about paying for this little lot..." Tommy put a hand in his pocket.

"Nonsense!" Agatha declared at once. "This is my treat for you being such an understanding listener."

"But really..."

"I insist. This is the Twentieth Century, Tommy, and a girl can pay for a man's tea and cake if she jolly well pleases."

The grin of pleasure this rebuke caused Tommy, made Annie feel all a-tremble inside. She had never made such a grand gesture, in truth, she had never been able to afford it. Nor had she ever thought of paying for a man's food. Her mother would have been appalled, though probably Clara would think nothing of it. And that was when the realisation hit her; Agatha was rather like Clara, a modern woman fascinated by crime and the seedier parts of life, and Tommy was smitten with her. Of course he was! She was a woman who appealed to his mind. Annie bit her lip. How on earth could she compete with that?

The arrangements made, the party broke up. Agatha had more work to do at the library. She was determined to take something of value away from her trip to Brighton. Tommy said his goodbyes and said he would look forward to four o'clock. Annie somehow managed to hiss out a farewell as she pushed Tommy's chair outdoors. The February cold bit into them as they exited the warm teashop and Annie made a fuss of seeing that Tommy's coat and scarf was best arranged to keep him warm. At least that was something she could do, she doubted Agatha would worry about whether his scarf was neatly knotted. She didn't notice how frustrated Tommy was growing – he disliked being treated like an invalid.

They set off down the road, Annie walking more briskly than normal. Her mind was whirring as they reached the corner. She could hold her tongue no longer.

"Why did you have to ask that woman to tea?" she demanded.

"She wants to meet Clara," Tommy said innocently.

"Supposing Clara doesn't want to meet her? She is very busy at the moment. She might appreciate to eat her tea in peace, rather than have some busy-body asking a lot of questions."

Tommy didn't answer at first. When he did his tone was clipped.

"That was an unpleasant thing to say, Annie."

Annie caught her breath. The mistake seemed to linger between them.

"I'm sure she is perfectly nice," she said, meaning it as an apology, but the words came out hard-edged and sounded like another insult.

"What is the matter with you Annie? Last night you were belittling Oliver, today you are rude about my new friend."

"It's nothing."

They walked on in silence.

"I'm sorry," Annie said after a while, this time her words were genuine.

Tommy did not respond. The walk home was painfully quiet.

Chapter Ten

Mrs Uxbridge was a small woman of around seventy who had worn 'widow's weeds' for the last twenty years, ever since her husband had died. She looked like a relic from another age in her Edwardian black gown and mourning jewellery. But she was a pleasant hostess, who saw instantly that Clara was tired and a little out-of-breath from her long walk (Clara had had to run most of the last half mile to make sure she reached Mrs Uxbridge in time for their appointment. This had not been easy in dress shoes), and sat her in a chair, before fetching a jug of the most exquisite lemonade. It turned out that Mrs Uxbridge devoted her life to food and drink, which for one so painfully thin was surprising. Mrs Uxbridge rarely ate or drank any of the things she made, but she was a prolific and proficient cook nonetheless. Her Dundee cake was highly regarded at the Church fete, and she made ends meet by providing simple wedding breakfasts to couples on a budget. Her finger sandwiches were, apparently, to die for.

Needless to say, it was Mrs Uxbridge's culinary talents that had roused the jealous monster within the poison pen writer. Mrs Uxbridge had destroyed the letter in a fit of uncharacteristic fury, when a batch of currant buns had burned in the oven unexpectedly. Up until that point, she had thought to keep it as evidence.

"I almost went to the police," Mrs Uxbridge explained. "Somehow I couldn't bring myself to do it. Things like that upset you a great deal when you are all alone with no one to confide in."

Mrs Uxbridge stared at her lemonade; she was a very sad figure who had never come to terms with being made a widow in her fifties. Mr Uxbridge had been her life. She had spent endless hours cooking for him; it had been her greatest pleasure. Then he was gone and, with no children to dote on, she found herself lost and unsettled. Her outlet had, yet again, been cooking. This time it was for her husband's wake. But when she received so many complements for her efforts, she began to wonder about doing something else. There was the summer fete coming up, after all, and the church jumble sale. Before long Mrs Uxbridge had thrown herself once more into baking for others, and it had brought her great comfort, and even a little income, over the last two decades.

"It said things about my cakes that no one should ever say," Mrs Uxbridge grew stiff. "That letter was the work of the Devil himself."

"What exactly did it say?"

"It accused me of things. I should explain. You are probably too young to remember, but, back in 1906, there was a dreadful cholera outbreak in the town. It was eventually traced back to one water pump used extensively by several households, but not before there had been a number of deaths. You are, no doubt, aware of how deadly cholera can be?"

Clara indicated she was.

"I remember it was one of those whispered words during my childhood," Mrs Uxbridge continued. "Whenever someone was sick with a stomach complaint, especially a child, it was dreaded it might be cholera. No matter if you had your own pump or lived in the smartest of houses with piped water, the worry still hung over you.

Many people were not sure how it was spread, and that added to the agony. People drank contaminated water without realising it would make them sick. I really can't emphasise enough the dread the disease caused to anyone living in a town or city. When someone was diagnosed with the sickness, panic would follow.

"But I am rambling," Mrs Uxbridge apologised. "I merely wanted you to understand the context of the accusations and why that letter caused me such pain. Cholera is a hated word among people of my generation. In any case, I must return to 1906, and the outbreak that swept through a number of the poorer families in the town. Two of its many victims happened to be a recently wedded couple, Mr and Mrs Miles. They were a lovely couple. He was a labourer on a farm and she used to walk the beach combing for anything of value. Her family had been beach combers for generations. It was a hard life, but they were content and happy, and they had none of the harshness that can seep into people who have to scrape a living. I liked them the first time I met them."

A smile came on Mrs Uxbridge's face.

"They reminded me of myself and my husband, Bill, all those years ago. I met them at a church function. I had prepared a buffet for the ladies' choral society, and it so happened that Mrs Miles – well, she was Miss Brown then – was a member. She approached me very quietly about what I would charge for a wedding cake. I am extremely soft-hearted, and I saw at once the poor dear did not have a lot of money to spend, so I asked her how much could she spare? Well, it wasn't much. Just enough for the ingredients, really. She said she would make do with a façade cake, do you know what that is?"

"I believe it is when a cardboard box in the shape of a large wedding cake is iced to look like the real thing. When, in fact, beneath the box, is a small sponge cake," Clara suggested.

"Indeed, I have made several of those before now. They look the part, but are a great deal cheaper. But, you see, I liked Miss Brown and her fiancé, and, back then, I had not done many wedding cakes and fancied the challenge. Most people went to the bakery on the corner of West Street for their wedding cakes. So, I said I was sure I could make the cake of her dreams for the little she could afford. A slight lie, I suppose, but nothing evil about it."

"Not at all," Clara agreed.

"And that is what I did. I made a square fruit cake and I iced it with marzipan and white royal icing. Oh, it looked beautiful! I even iced on the date of the wedding, and a little verse about wedded bliss. When Miss Brown saw it she almost cried, and thanked me from the bottom of her heart. She pressed an invitation to the wedding and the reception into my hand, and kissed me on the cheek," Mrs Uxbridge's eyes sparkled with tears. "It was a wonderful day. So much laughter and happiness. It seems so awful now, when I think on it, that that joy should have ended in death a mere week later. The wedding was on the Saturday. Mr Miles was taken ill on the Sunday night. The couple had just moved into Mr Miles' parents' house, which happened to have its water supplied by the affected pump. At first we imagined he had overindulged at the wedding, everyone was too joyous to think otherwise. But then he became worse, and other people in the neighbourhood sickened too. The doctor came and diagnosed cholera. He told everyone to only drink boiled water and he had the pump water tested. But it was already too late.

"Mrs Miles was already sick. She tended her new husband as long as she could, then she was taken so ill she was confined to bed. There was talk of taking them to the hospital, but money was so tight and hospitals cannot do much for cholera. By the following Saturday young Mr Miles was dead and his wife followed shortly after. They say she had shown signs of improvement, but when she heard her husband was gone she simply closed her eyes and wasted away. I remember the funeral so vividly. They were buried together. I did the food for the wake. It was the best I could do, as a gesture of my deep sympathy."

"That is very sad," Clara said. "But what do two deaths from cholera fifteen years ago have to do with the letter you received?"

"Because of what they wrote in it," Mrs Uxbridge looked astonished, as if Clara had asked an absurd question. "The letter implied that Mr and Mrs Miles did not die from cholera at all, but from arsenic that I had laced their wedding cake with! Can you imagine anything more hurtful? To accuse me of murder is one thing, but to imply I poisoned one of my own cakes? I take great care and pride over my cooking, Miss Fitzgerald, I can't think of a more ghastly thing anyone could say to me."

"How curious, the letter writer referred to events that had happened in 1906? That means the person behind the letter has been in Brighton a considerable time, to remember the deaths of the Mr and Mrs Miles. Have you contemplated who the writer might be?"

"Many people know I make cakes and, I dare say, a large number of them are aware I made the wedding cake for the Miles' marriage. I have no one specific in mind."

"Is there anyone you can think of, who you might have unintentionally upset in the last few months?"

"I am not that sort of person!"

"No, no. But perhaps someone has taken offence over something you could not help. People do sometimes."

Mrs Uxbridge gave a sniff, implying she did not like the idea that she made enemies, but considered the question nonetheless.

"I cannot think of anyone. No one has a complaint against me..." she hesitated. "Unless someone dislikes my cooking?"

Mrs Uxbridge looked mortified, as if her world had crumbled a little around her.

"I am sure that is not the case," Clara said quickly. "I merely meant that some people take grudges over the silliest of things."

"Hmm, yes, I suppose. Like the Cotterley sisters across the road," Mrs Uxbridge pointed out of her window to the house opposite. "They are poor old souls who never leave their house these days. Oh, but look in their front garden by accident and you'll be accused of spying on them. Knock on their door to pay a visit and you will be called an interfering busybody who wants to know all their business! Really, they are so determined to isolate themselves."

Mrs Uxbridge tutted.

"Could they...?" Clara began.

Mrs Uxbridge stopped her with a laugh.

"My dear, they don't leave the house. Besides, I hear tell they received a letter too. But heaven help anyone trying to find out what was in it. Best leave them to their own misery."

Despite Mrs Uxbridge's denial, Clara made a note to keep the Cotterley sisters in mind as suspects. For the time being, they were the only candidates she had.

"Well, thank you Mrs Uxbridge."

Clara took her leave. On the street outside, she took a good look at the Cotterley house. A wizened face appeared suddenly at the window and scowled back at her. What had Clara said about the letter writer being bitter and vindictive? And what of Tommy's suggestion that there was more than one person behind the cruel notes? She met the mean look in the eyes of the wizened face. It suddenly retreated. Clara felt a new door opening into her investigation.

Chapter Eleven

Clara ate lunch in a local pub that had a women's room. Clara's suffragette leanings resented being shunted into a separate room just because she was female, but she did enjoy the peace and quiet. She indulged in a Ploughman's; thick brown bread, cheese, raw onion, a slice of gammon, pickles and an apple that had survived the long winter stored in a cellar. She ate slowly and thought hard. What connection could she make between the Cotterley sisters and the other recipients of the letters? And how could she explain the letters being taken to the town post office, a considerable distance from the Cotterley residence, if the ladies never went outdoors? Just as importantly, how was she to get an audience with the sisters? She still needed to know more. Clara finished her lunch and headed for her next appointment – Mr Vincenzo at no.29.

Igio Vincenzo was Italian. He spoke with a light Sicilian accent and welcomed Clara into a house that was airy and sparsely furnished. Mr Vincenzo liked space, and he refrained from keeping the clutter that over-crowded most of the houses in Brighton. Mr Vincenzo owned a smart restaurant in the better part of town. It opened at seven o'clock and did not close until midnight. That was why he was home during the day.

He smiled at Clara's arrival, kissed her on both cheeks, and showed her into a back room that overlooked a very small, but incredibly well-tended, garden. He ushered her to a chair and without another word vanished, only to return with a plate of glistening cakes. He offered a dainty pastry to Clara and she felt it impolite to refuse. The twist of puff pastry had been fried and coated in sugar. It tasted divine and unlike anything Clara had ever eaten before.

"You are a very good cook," Clara complemented the Italian.

Vincenzo flung his hands up heavenwards.

"I should hope so. Mama would be disappointed if I was not. She taught me when I was just a little boy."

"What brought you to England, Mr Vincenzo?"

"War," Vincenzo shrugged. "Not the last one. My father decided to leave Italy when there was such strife over unification. Dear General Garibaldi was trying to make the country better, but all my father saw was conflict and bloodshed. So he brought his family to England."

"Then you were raised in England?"

Vincenzo gave another big shrug,

"I've never even been to Italy," he laughed. "But mama taught me how to cook properly, not like English food. Forgive me, but I cannot stand roast beef, it is so soulless."

Clara, who was personally fond of roasts, let this comment pass.

"Can I ask about the letter? I have read it, naturally."

Vincenzo gave a laugh that sounded a little forced.

"How stupid was that letter? I read it and I think, what stupid person has written this? It says I am a foreigner who should go back to where he came from. I was born in England! I am living where I came from. Ah!" he threw up his hands in despair, it seemed this gesture was his favourite and could mean a variety of things.

"Were you angry when you read it?"

"I was disappointed. Anger is wasted on such things. I

get angry when my chef overcooks the pasta, or I can't find decent tomatoes. Anger is best saved for important things, like that."

"And have you ever considered who sent it?"

Vincenzo gave his most dramatic shrug.

"Someone who doesn't like foreigners?" he offered.

The Vincenzo interview had been rather disappointing and Clara found herself having to dawdle outside to waste time before her appointment with Mr and Mrs Summerton. She found a corner shop selling an array of magazines, including several from America. Before she knew it she was ordering a subscription to 'Horrid Crimes!' a US publication that, despite its gory title, had several good pieces of journalism on crime detection and psychology inside. She saw it as something Tommy would enjoy reading; he was always going on about American detectives and their wily tricks for catching criminals. This was the problem, Clara reflected as she pulled coins out of her purse, with having too much time to waste; it tempted you to spend money. She toyed in the shop a little longer, contemplating buying a fashion magazine featuring some patterns for new dresses, when she heard a noise outside.

Clara glanced up at the shopkeeper who was leaning as far over his counter as he could manage to see out of his shop window.

"Mr Summerton again," he said in a tone of resignation. "Now what is the matter today?"

Clara didn't ask for further details, she was too busy darting for the door to get outside and see what was going on. Mr Summerton was in the middle of the street yelling at a young lad driving a pony and cart.

"And that is what is wrong with this world!" he was shouting, while one irate finger pointed down at a large, steaming, pile of manure the boy's pony had just deposited. "We have lovely clean streets and the likes of you go along messing them up! Do you know the sickness that can cause? We have to think of our health! You will clean it up, at once!"

The lad was clearly shaken by this tirade. He half fell off his cart in his haste to obey Mr Summerton's barked order. His cart was full of coal, and it happened that he had several empty sacks lying on top of his cargo. He grabbed the shovel he used for loading and unloading coal, and scooped up the manure into a sack. Then he looked timidly at Mr Summerton, waiting for a further command.

"Well? Take it away then!"

The lad threw his shovel and sack back onto the cart and scurried up onto his seat. He clicked the pony's reins so fast Mr Summerton barely had time to spring out of the way before the cart was rolling along again. The boy cast one nervous look back at the belligerent man, before hurrying to the end of the road.

Clara walked over to Mr Summerton quite calmly. He was just returning from work. He still had on his apron. Clara recalled being told he was a general grocer with a shop down by the quay. He turned to her with an angry look, then realised who she was and mellowed.

"It's a disgrace," he muttered, almost apologetically. "Look how clean we keep this road."

He gestured along the street which was, indeed, very neatly swept.

"I helped form a committee to pay for someone to sweep the roads every day," Mr Summerton said proudly. "Our idea was highly commended. You see, there is this lad who has not got all his marbles. His parents wanted to find him some work to keep him busy, but no one wanted him. And then I said, what if we paid him to keep the roads swept? Kills two birds with one stone, that. Do you know how much disease is caused by filth and rubbish left in our streets? It pollutes the air and causes people to become ill. I learned that in hospital during the war."

Mr Summerton gave a decisive nod of his head to punctuate the point.

"Then you get people like that boy coming along and

messing it all up without thinking," he snorted. "I'm not just thinking about myself, mind. My wife needs the best air possible while she is expecting, and the baby will too, when its born. I'm thinking of the children."

"I understand completely," Clara assured him. "I happen to be a little early, but if you wanted to commence our appointment..?"

"Come this way at once, Miss Fitzgerald. It will only take me a moment to change into some decent clothes. My wife will make you a cup of tea."

He escorted Clara along the road to his house. As Clara had expected, his front garden was exceptionally neat and arranged with small shrubs.

"Lemon balm, rosemary and that there is lavender," Mr Summerton informed her as he opened the gate. "All herbs that sweeten the air and create a soothing atmosphere. Very restorative."

He opened the front door and called out,

"Rosalind!"

There was a rustle of papers from further down the hall, and the heavily pregnant Rosalind tottered through a doorway, a magazine still clutched in one hand.

"Rosalind, Miss Fitzgerald is a little early. Make her comfortable, won't you, while I get changed."

Without another word, Mr Summerton headed for the stairs and left Clara alone in the hallway with Mrs Summerton. Rosalind gave a shy smile and a slight shrug, then she motioned for Clara to follow her back into the room she had just left.

It proved to be a snug sitting room, with a fire burning gently in the grate and magazines strewn everywhere. Mrs Summerton was clearly an avid reader.

"Take a seat," she said. "Would you like tea?"

"Only if you let me help you make it," Clara responded.

"Oh," Rosalind looked a little flustered. "Well, I suppose so."

She led the way back into the hall and towards the kitchen at the end of the house.

"When are you due?" Clara asked.

"Next month," Rosalind gave a wry grin. "It won't be soon enough. My ankles and feet are so swollen I hardly fit any of my shoes."

"Is this your first?"

"Yes. Joshua, my husband, is delighted. We weren't sure we could have children when he came back from the war. He was gassed, you see, and no one really knows what that does to a man, not even the doctors."

Clara began to understand Mr Summerton's obsession with clean air.

"Well, congratulations."

"Thank you," Rosalind beamed with pleasure. "Do you have children? Oh no, but of course, you are a 'miss'."

Rosalind blushed, feeling she had just made a dreadful social faux pas.

"I don't, no," Clara told her.

"I always say the wrong thing. I am dreadful for it. Joshua tells me I must think before I open my mouth."

"Really, it is of no matter," Clara smiled. "It was a natural enough question."

They finished making the pot of tea and Clara carried the tray of tea things back to the sitting room. Mrs Summerton gave the fire a hearty stir with the poker, and then settled with a groan into a chair.

"No one told me how tiresome having a baby was," She sighed gently. "Everything is such a chore."

"It will be over soon enough."

"Oh yes, and then I really will be tired!" Rosalind giggled to herself. "I know that part, my friends are all keen to tell me how they spend most of their nights awake listening for baby. Joshua worries about me so much, he even suggested we hire a nanny! How could we possibly afford that? But, bless him for being so concerned for me."

Rosalind gave Clara a theatrical wink.

"I'm tougher than I look," she added.

"I'm sure of it," Clara smiled.

Just then Joshua returned. He glanced at the two women seated and drinking tea, and felt a little uncertain about intruding. He suddenly felt out of place.

"Joshua, do come and sit down," Rosalind glanced up at her husband.

Joshua settled into the remaining armchair and looked a little apprehensively at Clara.

"You know about the contents of the letter we received?"

The blustering, gruff man from outside had suddenly dwindled into a quiet, nervous creature. Clara found the change quite surprising. Out of his business clothes, Mr Summerton had become anxious and uncomfortable in her presence. It turned out that in many ways he was as shy and socially awkward as his wife.

"Yes. I don't believe it for an instant."

"Good. To infer that Rosalind had been cavorting with another man…" Mr Summerton bit his lip. "There was talk, you see, when I came home, that my injuries might make having children a problem. I was gassed and nearly died. I'm one of the lucky ones. My lungs are not so good, which is why my old boss left me the grocery business when he retired. He didn't know who to pass it on to, you see, and he knew I would need an inside job with only light lifting. It was very kind of him. Even so, I have to be careful this time of year not to become ill, it could turn into pneumonia. I came home in 1917, I didn't look so good then, my body was broken."

"He had this awful yellow tinge to his skin," Rosalind piped up. "It was ghastly."

"Yes, and, of course, we hadn't been married long before I left for the front. Just a couple of months. When I came back, well, people assume the first thing a young married couple does is have children, but when three years passed with no sign of Rosalind… well… the rumours began."

"In a road like this people gossip constantly," an angry look had appeared on Rosalind's face. "It is as if they have nothing better to do."

"Perhaps they don't?" Clara suggested slyly.

"We knew what they were saying, naturally," Joshua added. "I can't say I wasn't hurt, but at the same time I was happy with Rosalind, and I wasn't going to let anyone spoil that for me. We moved to Brighton when we were first married because I was offered a job at Carter's General Grocery and we wanted to be in a town rather than in the countryside. Towns have more opportunities."

"And better schools," Rosalind nodded.

"So, we married and we moved here, but within a month I had my letter to say I was to go into the army. It was awful. I had to go to my boss and explain. I thought the man would be furious when I showed him the letter, but he said 'you've got something more important to do now, lad, than stacking boxes' and gave me his blessing. He is a very good man, Mr Carter. He promised to keep an eye on Rosalind and he did."

"He called in once a week, on a Sunday, to make sure I was all right and to hear the news on Joshua," Rosalind filled in her portion of the story. "He had three sons at the front and his wife had taken it hard. I think he liked to talk with someone about it. He would bring over the letters from his boys and we would read them together. He lost two of them, you know, and the third son came home without an arm."

Rosalind fell silent, a haunted look creeping over her face. Those had been long years, anxiously exchanging news on a Sunday, feeling temporary relief that for one more week everyone was safe. And then the bombshell of the losses.

"I think that is what started the gossip," she said at last. The angry look returned to her face. "It was so unkind. To infer we were misbehaving, when all we were doing was trying to bring a little hope and comfort to one another. I had no friends here then, who was I to talk to about Joshua? Those old gossips in the road? Oh, they would have loved to hear all about his doings at the front, but I refused to give them the satisfaction. I knew I could talk to Mr Carter, and he would listen sympathetically and say nothing to anyone else. I couldn't believe the cruelty of people."

"Then, when I came back, he offered me the business, despite that I had only been working for him a couple of months. People thought that was suspicious too," Joshua sighed sadly. "Mr and Mrs Carter still come round for tea on a Sunday. I refuse to let peoples' twisted minds spoil our friendship."

"But when three years passed and there was no baby, people started to say that Joshua was too sick or that something worse than gas had happened to him on the front. I thought it would all stop when I discovered I was expecting, but what a fool I was! People started saying instead that I must be carrying Mr Carter's child, that there was an understanding between us and Joshua, which is why he was given the business. I have never felt so disgusted and sickened!" Rosalind suddenly let out a small sob, the humiliation of the gossip had been unbearable, especially after all she had been through; the worry, the uncertainty. No one could tell her if Joshua would survive his first winter home, and then there had been the terrible influenza outbreak. She had lived constantly on edge, lest he catch the disease and die.

Joshua reached out for his wife's hand and squeezed it.

"Can you see why that letter made me so angry? To see all those rumours laid out in black and white. Rosalind read it and fell to pieces. I was scared we might lose the baby."

"We have done nothing wrong, Miss Fitzgerald, so why do they hate us?" Rosalind gave an exasperated cry.

"They don't hate you," Clara said calmly. "They just bored, silly people, who have little else in their lives to occupy themselves than scandal. Besides, I don't suppose all your neighbours were involved."

"No, no, that is true," Rosalind took a shaky breath. "It is really only a handful, and I have now made friends here."

"We won't let this nonsense drive us away," Joshua Summerton said firmly.

"Good," Clara smiled at them both. "Now, do you have any thoughts on who sent the letter?"

Rosalind glanced at Joshua, he just shook his head.

"I thought I did, but I was wrong," he said.

"Who did you suspect?" Clara asked.

Joshua gave a humourless laugh.

"Mrs Wilton! But then she received a letter too. She is one of the worst gossips in town."

Clara couldn't deny that. Mrs Wilton was always so busy interfering in other peoples' business that she had no time to take care of her own.

"Do you know the Cotterley sisters?" she asked after a moment.

"Oh, they live down the road," Rosalind said. "You never see them. They are recluses. I don't think they ever have visitors. One has a daughter who brings their shopping, but she only stays as long as she must. Have they received a letter?"

"I couldn't say," Clara lied. "Their name came up, that is all. I wondered if it was important."

"I don't think I have ever even spoken to them," Rosalind added.

"They did send a letter once, to the Clean Streets Committee I founded, stating their wholehearted support for the scheme. I believe they even donated a ha'penny," Joshua said.

"They are mean too," Rosalind nodded. "Though, perhaps they are just poor. I hear they live on nothing but cabbage, potatoes and a little liver."

"I don't suppose you still have the letter they sent to the committee?" Clara was thinking that a comparison between the two missives might prove enlightening.

"It will be with the committee papers. The Chairman looks after that. We elected Reverend Harding for the role."

Clara knew the name. The conversation came to a natural lull and it was clear there was no more to be discovered from the Summertons. Clara thanked them for their time and honesty and excused herself. As she headed for home, she once more glanced in the direction of the Cotterley house. Yet again there was someone in the window peering out at her. The expression on their face was not friendly. Clara gave them a wave anyway, she had nothing to hide. The face vanished from sight and a net curtain swung into its place. Clara shook her head. Strange, strange people. After such a long day she was really looking forward to a quiet evening at home.

Chapter Twelve

"Heavens, I hope there is a large pot of tea ready, Annie. I feel I have walked a marathon distance. My feet are killing me and I am absolutely…" Clara stepped into the parlour and spotted an unfamiliar woman in her favourite armchair, "…exhausted."

Clara turned her head to Tommy who was looking a touch embarrassed. Agatha had arrived spot on time, but his sister had run late, and it was now close to five o'clock. Annie had made an effort to suppress her jealously and be exorbitantly nice to their guest, but after forty-five minutes of bravado, the façade was wearing thin.

"May I introduce…"

"Agatha."

Tommy and Agatha spoke at once. Clara looked at one, then the other, before walking forward and shaking the hand Agatha offered.

"Agatha..?" Clara asked.

"Christie," Agatha smiled. "But please use my Christian name, I find it less formal."

"Clara," Clara said.

"Agatha is a mystery writer," Tommy quickly explained. "Down in Brighton doing some research for her next book. She wanted to meet a real detective."

"Oh?" Clara said. "And where would you find one of those in Brighton?"

Agatha was amused.

"You are too modest, Miss Fitzgerald, or may I call you Clara?"

"You may," Clara started to pull the scarf from around her neck. "Will you excuse me a moment while I take off my coat and fetch myself a cup of tea?"

"Of course."

Clara exited back into the hall and went in search of Annie, wondering just what had been going on in her absence. Who was Agatha and why on earth would she want to know about Clara? Clara felt a little embarrassed by it all, the woman had seemed quite delighted to see her, as if she was someone famous. It had quite flustered Clara.

She entered the kitchen and threw her coat over the back of a chair.

"Annie, who is this woman in the parlour?"

Annie had a face like thunder. Clara had always considered that an odd analogy, but seeing her friend's mood, she rapidly began to understand the allusion.

"That would be Agatha," Annie said with difficulty through the angry pout on her lips. "Tommy invited her."

Clara looked at her curiously.

"You don't like her?"

"What is there not to like?" Annie declared, her tone suggesting the complete opposite.

Clara was bamboozled. Why had Annie taken so against this woman?

"Has she been rude to you?"

"No. Perfectly polite."

"Then, what have I missed?"

Annie didn't answer, but handed Clara a cup of hot tea and a plate of sandwiches.

"You look done in. Go sit down and eat this," With that Annie stormed off to the pantry for potatoes, with no intention of returning until Clara was gone from the kitchen.

Clara made her way back down the hall, feeling a stranger in her own home. She had only been gone a few hours, yet it could have been years the way the world had changed around her. A stranger greeting her like an old friend, Annie in a dangerous temper. It was all so bizarre.

She came to the parlour and took a seat on the old sofa, which sagged in the middle and had a nasty tendency to erupt springs in the most inconvenient places.

"I won't keep you long Clara, for I can see you are tired. Perhaps, when you are less busy, I could pick your brains over a few things?" Agatha said.

"Really, it's no bother," Clara assured her, feeling she would rather get this meeting over and done with then have to arrange another time.

"Tommy has been telling me about some of your previous cases. From what I understand, you work as a team?"

"I am very much an assistant only," Tommy quickly said.

"Tommy does his fair share," Clara corrected him. "Without his assistance, and his ability to piece together puzzles, I would be lost."

"How fascinating," said Agatha. "And what are you working on at the moment?"

"I really couldn't say."

"No, no. Of course not. Now, tell me Clara, what is it like being a detective?" Agatha turned a very serious look on Clara. "I imagine it has its dark moments."

"That it does," Clara agreed. "It can be exhausting and frustrating, also there are times when you wished you had not solved a case."

"You feel some mysteries are best left unsolved?"

Clara hesitated. Was that what she meant?

"No, it's just... Digging around in peoples' lives often brings up secrets that are irrelevant to the case, but which nonetheless are revealed. If a person keeps a secret for a long time, invariably it is because it may hurt them or someone else. When it relates to a crime, I have no sympathy, but sometimes I feel investigating causes a lot of 'collateral damage', as the Americans put it."

"Rather like fighting a bloody war," Tommy interjected. "Even if it is being fought for the right reasons and you win, there are all those lives lost or damaged along the way that you can't do anything about. The outcome sometimes seems very costly."

"Do you feel like that with all your cases?" Agatha asked. She had become quieter, listening hard, imagining what it was like to be in Clara's shoes.

"No, not all cases. But very rarely is an ending entirely happy. After all, I am investigating a crime, which means someone has already been hurt. Sometimes irreparably. I can find it challenging, but I would rather I was doing it then someone who didn't care, who was just out for the money or the glory."

"I see," Agatha was quiet. "Clara, do you think a woman makes a better detective than a man? It is something I have been mulling over."

"No, not better," Clara smiled lightly. "Just different. Women think in a different way to men."

Clara ate a sandwich in the hush that followed. While she answered Agatha's questions her mind was still on the poison pen case and, of course, Brompton. She had hardly begun to unravel that mystery. She was also wondering how Oliver was.

"Well, I fear I have already taken up too much of your time," Agatha rose from her chair. "Thank you for talking to me, Clara. It has been most illuminating."

Agatha was seen to the door, and then Clara collapsed in her armchair and gave a sigh of relief. She kicked off her shoes, stretched out her stockinged feet and wriggled her toes.

"What were the Whites like?" Tommy asked her.

"Pleasant," Clara replied. "Oh, Mrs White gave me

this, thought it might be a clue."

Clara fudged in her handbag and produced the piece of chromed metal. She handed it to Tommy.

"It certainly looks like something off a car," she added.

Tommy turned it over in his hand.

"Part of the wheel trim, perhaps?" he suggested. "Do you want me to see what I can find out?"

"Do. By the way, did you find out about Colonel Fairbanks?"

"Oh yes, rather more than I wanted in fact," Tommy laughed. "I got his address out of the Post Office directory, and then I had this idea of calling Colonel Brandt at his club and seeing if he knew the man. Colonels tend to flock together, you know, especially when they end up in the same town."

"No doubt Colonel Brandt was pleased to help," Clara was fond of the Colonel who she had met on a previous case. He was a rather lonely old man who she regularly invited over for Sunday dinner. Colonel Brandt liked to talk about old times and the army, but he was a mine of information once you knew how to channel his train of thought in the right direction.

"Brandt always is. We had a long chat over the 'phone. I dare say that butler fellow they have in the Club lobby was getting agitated over how long we took! In any case, Colonel Brandt knew at once who I meant, because Fairbanks is a member of the Club too, though he doesn't visit all that often, perhaps once or twice a month. Brandt has played golf with him on a few occasions – claims he cheats, by the way," Tommy grinned. "Brandt says the old boy retired from the Met around 1911 and moved down to Brighton for the sea air. But he hasn't quite been able to give up policing and has been known to interfere in local cases. Not so much recently though, for his health has deteriorated. He lives alone in a pretty villa and has a passion for model aeroplanes. He was involved in the Jack the Ripper case, you know."

"It wouldn't surprise me," Clara answered. "Though,

not a case the police wish to boast about, considering Jack got away."

"Colonel Brandt was a bit uncertain of what exactly was wrong with Fairbanks, he thought it might be lung or heart related. He served in Africa before he became a policeman. Those were the days when an army man could almost guarantee himself a decent position in the police force when he gave up on shooting people. Apparently, Fairbanks rose through the ranks pretty swiftly and was good at his job too."

"Is he liable to be too ill to speak with me?"

"Brandt didn't think so, more a case that he doesn't travel far from home."

"So, another piece of the puzzle. Is he on the telephone?"

"There was no number in the directory."

"I shall write him a letter then. Tommy, what is wrong with Annie?"

Tommy gave a groan.

"She dislikes Agatha," Tommy dropped his voice to a whisper. "For some absurd reason she is jealous of her, seems to think I am about to run off with her."

Tommy indicated the craziness of this idea by gesturing at his wheelchair.

"Oh dear," Clara sighed. "Best we all watch what we say then."

Clara almost jumped out of her skin as Annie then appeared in the doorway.

"Is she gone?"

"You can see that Annie, else you wouldn't ask," Tommy gave her a wink. "She has gone away to plot out the best time for our elopement."

Clara kicked Tommy hard on the shin.

"Ow!"

"You can be horrid Thomas Fitzgerald," Annie said with a hurt sniff. "I shall serve dinner now."

"You are a fool," Clara snapped at him, as soon as Annie was gone.

"I was only teasing!"

"You don't have even half an idea how women think or feel," Clara 'tsked' at him. "The sooner you apologise the better."

Tommy looked sullen.

"After dinner," he said.

Clara glowered at him.

"Fine!" Tommy took hold of the wheels of his chair and awkwardly negotiated his way out of the room.

Clara watched his retreating figure and found she was smiling to herself. She closed her eyes and sank into the chair a little further. What was it with men and misunderstanding women? One thing she knew for sure, the quality of her dinner would heavily rely on harmony between Tommy and Annie. When Annie was in a temper she was prone to burning things. She was just hopeful Tommy could repair the damage before Annie's first class dumplings suffered the consequences.

Chapter Thirteen

After writing a letter to Colonel Fairbanks, Clara made her way on Thursday morning to the police station. She was going to go through the files on Brompton's accident and, if she was lucky, have a word with Constable Alfie Ling. The sergeant on the desk was his usual grumpy self when he saw her. She showed him her special pass-card, issued by Inspector Park-Coombs, and he had to let her through, though he didn't look pleased about it.

The archives room had been moved into the basement since the last time Clara had used it, and she had to trudge down concrete steps and find the light switch, before entering a room where a naked bulb hummed as it hung from the ceiling. She stared around at the racks of files and boxes. Everything had yet to be sorted into its correct place, and there were several piles of cardboard folders sitting on a long table. Clara really hoped Brompton's file was not among them.

She started to follow the alphabetical ordering on the racks. As she came to the corner of a stack, she almost stumbled across a man crouched on the floor. Clara found herself just looking at the man for several moments, before it dawned on her that he might be dead. He was a policeman, certainly, the uniform told her that much. But there was a nasty swelling on his head just above the left temple, and he didn't seem to be breathing. It was several more moments before Clara realised she was looking at James Brompton. He was in his old constable's uniform. But why was he here, crouched over a box with a bump on his head the size of a chicken's egg? There was no time to waste; Clara bent down and felt for a pulse. Brompton was breathing, but it was shallow and uneven. Clara looked around her for any sign of what might have happened. She was fairly certain this was no accident. Brompton had come here for a reason and the way he was crouched near a box of files suggested he had been looking for something, but what? The box had a slip on the front that indicated it came from the 'C' section. If Brompton was looking for his own file and details of his accident, he wouldn't find it in this box.

Clara took another look around the room. She had to fetch help, but she wasn't prepared to leave Brompton alone in a room where his attacker might still lurk. She could not see anyone among the stacks. After a further moment's hesitation she ran for the archives door and darted into the corridor. In the same instant Alfie Ling appeared from nowhere and collided with her.

"Miss Fitzgerald?"

"Constable Ling, call for a doctor at once and send Inspector Park-Coombs down here!"

Alfie Ling blinked at her, uncomprehending.

"At once Ling, at once!" Clara commanded in her most authoritative tone, her fears for Brompton overriding any concerns she might have at speaking to an officer of the law in such a way.

Ling blinked again, looking like a confused mole that had just popped its head above ground. Then he came to a decision and ran for the stairs out of the basement. Clara returned to Brompton and sat down beside him. What was he doing here? And in his old uniform too? Well, perhaps the latter was fairly explainable. If someone wanted to get down to the archives of a police station, the easiest way to do so without attracting curiosity was to be in a police uniform. Brompton would have waited until the Desk Sergeant was suitably distracted, then walked passed him towards the back of the station. The busy Desk Sergeant might have glimpsed a blue uniform, but would have paid little attention to who was in it.

However, Clara had not suspected that the man she had met in the hospital filing room could be capable of such subterfuge. Could she have been mistaken? Clara wasn't sure. The one thing she had learned during her time as a detective, was that people were complicated and full of surprises. Suggesting you ever knew someone else absolutely was sheer arrogance, in her humble opinion.

Clara was relieved when the door to the archives opened and someone entered. Inspector Park-Coombs peered around the stacks.

"Clara?"

"It's Brompton again."

The Inspector came around the shelving and stared in disbelief at the crouched man on the floor.

"What is he doing here?"

"I suspect he was looking for something," Clara pointed to the box of files in front of the injured constable. "As you can see, someone has taken another swing at him. But I think they were disturbed before they could kill him, perhaps even by my arrival, though I saw no one in here when I entered."

"There is another door at the far end," Park-Coombs said, indicating towards the far side of the room with a finger. "They may have slipped out that way as you came in."

Clara pursed her lips, contemplating how she had raced into the corridor and bumped straight into Alfie Ling. Was Annie right, after all, and the troublesome child had grown up to be a dangerous man.

"The doctor is on his way," The Inspector knelt by Brompton and peered into the man's face. "Clara, I would like you to leave, this needs to be dealt with as police business only."

Clara didn't speak at once. She waited for the Inspector to look up at her.

"You asked for my help."

"I know, but this situation has taken a nasty turn. If someone is prepared to attack a constable in a police station, then I can hardly ensure your safety, can I?"

"You forget. I have a vested interest in finding who is responsible too. Someone in your station allowed Billy 'Razor' Brown to escape and come after me. I could have been killed or badly hurt. I am not inclined to ignore that fact."

"I don't want to see you hurt Clara. I shall speak with my superiors and have a proper investigation put in place."

"And send the culprit to earth?" Clara cocked her head to one side. "Not to mention risking your own position. Your superiors will likely transfer you."

"If not force me to retire for allowing such a mess in the first place."

"Precisely, and then where shall I be? The new Inspector may not be so accommodating to my snooping," Clara fixed the Inspector with her most firm and determined stare. "You have no option but to let me help, I won't allow you to cut me out of this case. We shall find the traitor and deal with him before wind of this reaches your superiors."

The Inspector was silent several moments, then he smiled.

"You already have a suspect in mind," he said.

"I do, but equally I could be wrong. I won't tarnish a man's reputation without good reason."

The conversation ended with the opening of the far door and the doctor arriving. The police doctor mainly dealt with drunks in the police cells, or brawlers with cuts and bruises. He was surprised at the scene that greeted him, and raised his bushy grey eyebrows before whistling through his teeth.

"What have we here then?"

The Inspector met Clara's stare, then turned to the doctor.

"Not entirely sure, but we think something fell on the constable's head as he was retrieving some files. A heavy box, maybe?"

The doctor squeezed between a stack of papers and managed to cause several brown files to flutter to the floor in the process. It was certainly a plausible excuse, considering the current untidy nature of the archive room. He dropped to one knee beside Brompton.

"Looks like a bump from hitting something hard, perhaps even the edge of one of these shelves. Your constable perhaps tripped, banged his head, and then crumpled backwards into this position," the doctor said.

"Quite probably," Park-Coombs agreed without hesitation. "I really must have some of our officers in here to tidy things up a bit."

"An accident waiting to happen," the doctor looked around him at the overloaded shelves and the stacks of files placed haphazardly on the floor. "I see this sort of thing all too often. Household accidents used to take up most of my time when I was in private practice. People place things down without thinking of the hazard they might cause."

The doctor tutted as he examined Brompton's head.

"Has he been conscious at all?"

"No," Clara answered.

The doctor looked at her for the first time, and his expression asked the unspoken question 'who are you'.

"Clara Fitzgerald," Clara offered a hand to shake. "I came down for a file."

"Clara does some outside work for the police," the Inspector added. "Background material and such."

The doctor looked unconvinced, but Brompton then groaned and provided the distraction they all needed.

"I've sent for an ambulance," The doctor turned back to the Inspector. "The constable who fetched me was not particularly enlightening on what the nature of the injury was, so I decided to play on the safe side of things."

"Very good."

"It should be here soon," The doctor rocked back on his heels. "However, I think he will come out of this with a bad concussion and nothing more serious. Tell him to be more careful in future."

The Inspector swore he would. They wasted some time in idle chat – the doctor providing a lengthy lecture on the general nature of head injuries – while awaiting the ambulance. Clara soon came to the conclusion the doctor's knowledge of anything more challenging than a bump or a scrape was decidedly limited. She supposed being a police doctor was rather a niche calling, and did not generally require much in the way of medical expertise. Anything more serious than a split lip or a cut forehead and the doctor would summon an ambulance and leave his patient in the care of the hospital. The doctor had no call to expand his quaint, old-fashioned knowledge of medicine; he had long since retired from private practice and being the police doctor supplemented his pension nicely, and provided the means to regularly enjoy the full social delights of the local golf club. Had the situation been different, Clara would have disliked the man for his ignorance, as it was, she was grateful for it. He didn't ask difficult questions and he accepted their explanations without hesitation, when another man might have been concerned.

When the ambulance finally came, Clara was glad to see Brompton's care being handed over to people with a little more sense. He was starting to rouse as they placed him on a stretcher and gingerly carried him upstairs.

"I shall give it an hour or two and then pop over to see him," Park-Coombs said as Brompton was taken away. "I'll need to pay a call on his parents first."

"I had assumed policemen gave back their uniforms when they were no longer part of the force?" Clara asked quietly.

"We let Brompton keep his because of the circumstances," Park-Coombs sighed. "I never expected to see him in it again."

Clara picked up the heavy box of files that had been at Brompton's feet and glanced inside. None of the names on the case files rang any bells. For a moment Clara almost found herself believing Park-Coombs explanation that Brompton had bumped his head by accident. Perhaps he had? Wasn't that possible? Then she shook off the idea. There were too many unanswered questions to consider this a case of pure coincidences. Brompton was down here for a reason. He was looking for something. She would visit him later and see if he could reveal anything, even just his reason for being down here. In the meantime, it was fast approaching the hour of her next appointment with one of the poison pen victims.

Clara said her farewells to Park-Coombs and headed out into another dull February day. What complicated lives people made for themselves, she was thinking, as she stepped onto the pavement and pulled up her coat collar in the face of the cold, whistling wind.

From behind her Alfie Ling appeared. It seemed he had been waiting for her.

"Will he be all right?" he asked Clara.

She turned sharply.

"Who?"

"Constable Brompton," Alfie wrung his hands together, they were red and swollen from the cold. "Will he be all right?"

"I don't know," Clara answered, an honest enough response.

Alfie gave her a nod of thanks then vanished inside the station. Clara watched him go, wondering how Alfie had known the man in the archives was former Constable Brompton without actually seeing him? She had been suspicious before, now she was even more so, as she headed off to see Miss Wicks about unpleasant letters.

Chapter Fourteen

Miss Wicks greeted Clara on her doorstep with the most disagreeable scowl imaginable.

"I have changed my mind about talking to you," the door rapidly closed in Clara's face.

Undeterred, Clara stood on the doorstep and rapped the knocker loudly. There was no answer.

"She is a humbug, that one."

Clara glanced to her right and saw a man leaning against Miss Wicks' garden wall. Miss Wicks lived in an end terrace and it was easy for the man to come around the corner and lean into the garden. He was a workman of some description, wearing a flat cap and a faded jacket, but his clean hands implied he did not work in a dirty industry.

"I would give up on that one. What are you trying to sell, anyway?"

"I am not selling anything," Clara told him, wondering if she looked like a door-to-door salesperson. "I had an appointment to speak with Miss Wicks concerning a private matter."

"The nasty letters?" the man asked.

Clara took another good look at him, but his face didn't ring a bell.

"My sister had one of those letters," he added, to explain how he knew about the matter. "Mrs Uxbridge."

"Oh," Now Clara looked, there was a slight resemblance between the man in the flat cap and the woman who had been accused of poisoning a wedding cake. "I see."

"No, you don't. You are wondering how I know about Miss Wicks. Well, I do some odd jobs for people around here and I laid some new linoleum for Miss Wicks a couple of weeks back. She might look a sour-faced creature, but everyone needs to talk sometimes, and it happened she talked to me."

Clara stepped off the doorstep and came closer to the man leaning on the wall.

"You are?"

"Matthew O'Donaghue. Carpenter by trade, but I do anything that pays the bills."

"Might you be able to suggest a way I can get Miss Wicks to speak to me?"

"Pick another day," O'Donaghue laughed at his own wit. "She has funny moods, that one. Today she will bite your head off. Tomorrow she will be as nice as an angel. But I can tell you about the letter she received."

Clara stared at him.

"Really?"

"I told you, when I laid her linoleum she chose to talk. I think the letter had just come and she needed to get things off her chest. Miss Wicks doesn't exactly have many friends."

Clara hesitated. Talking about Miss Wicks behind her back seemed unprofessional, yet the woman had simply refused to speak with her. Clara glanced back at the house.

"What precisely do you know?" she asked after a moment of indecision.

"Well, for a start, I read the letter," O'Donaghue grinned. "Some good stuff there was in it too. Buy me a cup of tea and I will tell you all about it."

Clara stared back at Miss Wicks' house yet again. Her better judgement told her to go away and call on the woman another day, but she was feeling impatient with the case, and Brompton was always on her mind. She wasn't sure she had time to deal with Miss Wicks' 'moods', or the patience. O'Donaghue was still grinning at her. A compromise was in order.

"I'll buy you a cup of tea and a sandwich if you persuade Miss Wicks to talk to me," she said.

O'Donaghue's smile faded.

"She won't."

"I sense you are a man who could charm blood out of a stone," Clara responded. "I think this is a perfect occasion for you to demonstrate your talents. Besides, you are the one she confided in."

O'Donaghue looked glum, but the promise of a free sandwich gave him the incentive to try his hand on the old battleaxe. He gave Clara a helpless look, then headed around the back of Miss Wicks' house, entering via the yard, to knock on the back door. Clara waited impatiently. It was cold in the front garden. A bitter wind was cutting down the street and buffeting everything in its path. Clara huddled in her coat, hoping O'Donaghue was already convincing Miss Wicks to welcome Clara inside. The time seemed to drag by, with Clara growing colder and colder. How could it be so difficult to help someone, after all? In any case, she had been asked here, it was not as if she had turned up unannounced. The only reason she was being so persistent was because, so far, clues as to who was writing the poison pen letters were few and far between. Miss Wicks might hold some nugget of information that would help, and even that felt like a vain hope. Had Clara been further forward in her case she would have just walked away, as it was, she was reluctant to let any potential lead elude her.

Her feet were numb by the time O'Donaghue reappeared looking sheepish.

"She reckons she will talk with you after all," he said.

"Now, that sandwich?"

Clara rummaged in her purse and handed him some money.

"Hear anything useful about these letters, Mr O'Donaghue, come see me," she handed him one of her cards too. "I'm sure I can stretch to more tea and sandwiches."

O'Donaghue took the card, grinning again.

"You can rely on me," he tugged the rim of his cap in a gesture of respect and then went off up the street whistling to himself.

Clara had to smile at the man's carefree attitude, not even a bitter February wind dinted his spirit. She headed through the back gate (deciding to assume she was not welcome at the front door) and found herself in Miss Wicks' extremely neat yard. Back yards, in Clara's experience, were not easy to maintain in military order. They tended to collect debris; things that needed to be thrown away, items awaiting fixing, or some other chore. They invariably retained a scruffy air, no matter how house proud the owner of the property was. In contrast, Miss Wicks' yard was alarmingly clean and, Clara mused for the right word, yes, sterile. The paving slabs were sparkling white, scrubbed within an inch of their lives. The brick walls were white-washed and reflected the grey daylight into brilliance. The space was almost empty otherwise. A washing line was wrapped in a neat bundle and hung on a hook on the wall, but aside from that there was not a bucket or broom, or any similar item one might find in someone's yard, in sight. Clara felt oddly exposed as she darted across the open space to Miss Wicks' back door.

The door was open a fraction and when Clara knocked on it, it swung open even further. She glanced into an extremely well-ordered kitchen. At a white pine kitchen table Miss Wicks sat with her back to Clara.

"You can come in," she said in a voice that made Clara feel more of an intruder than ever.

Clara entered the kitchen and quietly came around the table. Miss Wicks stared at her with cold eyes. She was in her fifties, a tall, spindly thing, who looked as if all the joy and pleasantness had been siphoned out of her long ago. Miss Wicks was like a shrivelled up lemon, sour and bitter beneath her waxen skin. She didn't offer Clara a chair, but Clara took one anyway. The two women stared at one another for some time, the only sound the idle ticking of a clock.

"You received a letter," Clara said, her patience gone.

"Yes."

"You didn't hand it over on the evening of the meeting so I could read it."

"No."

Clara felt she was pulling metaphorical teeth. She phrased her next question to require more than a single syllable answer.

"Why?"

Miss Wicks gave a haughty sniff

"It was private."

"You don't have to tell me the contents of the letter…"

"I know."

"…but, if the contents might provide a clue to the writer, I would suggest explaining them to me."

Miss Wicks looked extremely unamused by this suggestion.

"The only thing that letter could tell you, was that the person who wrote it was extremely unpleasant. Gossip is a sin, Miss Fitzgerald, and the writer of those letters is guilty of it. They will go to Hell, I am certain."

"Did you recognise the handwriting?"

"No."

"And the things it said, were they something anyone might know, or something very private?"

Miss Wicks hesitated at that, a chink in her armour had appeared.

"I couldn't say. I suppose it was a thing that people

could have imagined. There was no truth in the letter, naturally, but people will create such silly ideas in their heads."

"Were you upset by it?"

"I don't allow such nonsense to disturb me," Miss Wicks said a little too quickly. "Miss Fitzgerald, I really don't think I can help you."

"If I could see the letter…"

"Absolutely not!" Miss Wicks' eyes blazed with fury. "I don't need another busybody interfering in my business. It's just a silly letter."

"To you, maybe," Clara said calmly. "But others have been deeply upset by the things written in these letters. The person behind them must be stopped. I take this all very seriously."

"Then you are a fool. This is nothing but a silly game someone is playing."

Clara decided there was no point arguing further. She only had one card left to play.

"I don't suppose you know the Cotterley sisters?"

The question produced such a reaction in Miss Wicks, that Clara was almost startled. The sour, pale face grew red and awful, the eyes bulged and, when she spoke, Miss Wicks' voice had been narrowed to an irate hiss.

"Those women should be burned as witches!"

Clara could hardly mask her surprise.

"They are evil," Miss Wicks continued. "They have nothing good left in their souls."

"You are the first to say so."

"That is because I am one of the few who used to know them well," Miss Wicks drew a raspy breath. "I once thought of them as friends, until I realised how despicable they were. If you displease them, they turn on you like a pack of rabid dogs."

"Would you know their handwriting?"

Miss Wicks suddenly cocked her head on one side and looked at Clara curiously.

"If you are implying that they wrote that letter to me,

you are mistaken. It was not their handwriting, I know it well enough. Though, I suppose I could imagine them wicked enough to do such a thing."

Another dead end. Clara decided she had had enough of Miss Wicks' presence and excused herself. In the street again, she pulled her coat tight around her and wondered how one row of houses could collect such a strange assortment of souls. She checked her watch. There was around two hours before she had her appointment with Mrs Prinner; that was one interview she was looking forward to. Mrs Wilton believed Mrs Prinner knew something and her odd behaviour the other night certainly implied she was hiding something. Whether it was important or not, was another matter. Clara headed to the nearest teashop to warm herself and pass the time.

Chapter Fifteen

Being confined to a wheelchair sometimes made Tommy frustrated. He could not go where he pleased as other people did; he always needed someone to push him along, or help him up and down steps. There always seemed to be some challenge ahead, whether it was a narrow hallway or an awkward staircase. The world was not designed for people who could not walk, and yet now so many of Tommy's contemporaries were cripples, their agility taken away by four years of war. The old county cricket team was a sorry sight these days; half the players were invalids in some way. Bright, beautiful youth snatched away, to leave in its place prematurely old men, missing limbs, unable to walk, or gasping from gassed lungs. And those were only the ones whose wounds were visible; there were others whose scars ran deep inside and whose pain was mental rather than physical. Tommy felt they suffered the worst.

For a long time Tommy had avoided his old friends, too afraid to see his own traumas reflected in their faces. How did you look at a man you once laughed and cheered with now he was so different? Tommy used his own disabilities as an excuse. After all, it was hard for him to simply go to the pub or even take a stroll, and no one expected him to appear at the cricket ground, knowing the pain it would cause him. But, time was passing, and Tommy was beginning to see his personal retreat as something more harmful than protective. It was with this in mind that he began to think about Herbert Phinn.

Herbert was one of those boys who arrive at school wearing thick glasses, and who you know will spend most of the day being bullied by the more athletic lads who have yet to learn the value of intelligence. Herbert was a kind boy who tried to make friends through being generous with his sweets and pocket money, and who invariably ended up being hurt.

Tommy had recognised a lame duck as soon as he saw Herbert and took it upon himself to save the boy from the foxes who were crowding around ready to take a bite out of him. Back then, Tommy was the lad who was taller than everyone else, who could run the fastest and who knew how to fight with his fists. No one argued with Tommy once he took someone under his protection, be that his little sister or Herbert Phinn. Herbert repaid Tommy in the only way he knew how; he showed him everything he knew about science, for which he had an extraordinary passion. Herbert was very good at chemical experiments and had his own small laboratory kit, provided by a doting father. He refrained from making such childish things as stink bombs, but he could reanimate a dead frog using electricity and grow crystals in a dish. Everyone expected Herbert to become a chemist, and he didn't disappoint. The last time Tommy heard of him, he was off to university. That was five days before Tommy went to the front.

In the intervening years, Tommy had lost track of Herbert. He sometimes wondered if he was dead, like so many others. Had Herbert's genius died in a blaze of futile glory on the battlefield? Or perhaps he had dreamed of his last scientific experiments in some hospital bed, while he awaited death from war wounds?

With that in mind, it had taken Tommy by surprise to

open the crime magazine Clara had brought home for him, and to see staring back at him the round face of Herbert Phinn. He was even more surprised to learn that Herbert was back in Brighton, having finished a degree in chemistry. The magazine described him as a well-respected expect on poisonous substances and, even more importantly to Tommy, on handwriting. Apparently, Herbert had begun studying the subject of handwriting while at university. He had been experimenting with different ways of identifying various common pen inks using chemical tests, and had studied a number of friends' letters in the process. As he dabbled with chemical reactions, he started to become curious about the actual handwriting in the letters – the way the letters curled and curved, they were like chemical markers, all unique and able to identify their master. There were only a handful of handwriting experts in the country, but Herbert found one willing to tutor him and spent the next year learning all he could. The war intervened in his studies, in that ghastly way it was so able to, and for three years Herbert found himself dodging bullets and gas, while continuing his studies whenever he could. Chemistry was almost impossible in the trenches, but he could hone his skills in understanding handwriting by examining the letters his comrades received. He soon realised there was a great deal to be learned about the way a person put pen to paper.

Then he was home and he returned to his chemistry studies, but wind of his skills with handwriting got out and he was requested for help by a friend who was concerned that a relative's will had been forged. "The rest," Herbert told the magazine interviewer who spoke to him afterwards, "was history." Herbert was now being called a handwriting expert and, when he wasn't pursuing his passion for chemistry, he was in court giving testimony on who wrote what.

Tommy found himself smiling at the serendipitous nature of the article. Herbert Phinn, who would have thought it? Had Clara not had to waste time in a shop selling newspapers, had she not found this magazine and decided to buy it for him, had he not once upon a time taken a boy with thick glasses and no sense for survival whatsoever under his wing, then he never would have had the opportunity to get an expert to take a look at the poison pen letters.

Tommy wasted no time finding the telephone number for Herbert's parents. He knew they had a 'phone as they were very modern people, who liked to keep abreast of technology. He had heard that Herbert's father had even invested in a radio; a quite extravagant device that was virtually pointless, as there was only one radio station currently broadcasting, and that only played intermittent and extremely dull music. But Mr Phinn dreamed of the future and he believed the radio was the way forward. His neighbours might mock the great mahogany box that blared out tinny blasts of music, but Mr Phinn believed.

Tommy was grateful to anyone who was on the 'phone. It made life for him so much easier, seeing as he could not pay calls on people very easily, and sending messages via letters was such a drawn-out chore. He had rung Herbert's parents at once and introduced himself. They remembered him well and when he said he was hoping to speak with Herbert, they were only too delighted. They had promised to forward a message to their son and, within half-an-hour, Herbert was on the line, enthusiastically greeting his old friend.

They discussed old times and the terribleness of war for a while. Then Tommy explained how he had seen the article and described Clara's work, by the time he reached the part about the letters he could tell that Herbert was chomping at the bit to come over and take a look. He agreed to come at once, and Tommy had just enough time to ask Annie to nip out for some buns, before Herbert was on the doorstep, beaming at him.

Herbert had not changed. He was still the boy with the thick glasses who talked a little too much and who bubbled with enthusiasm. The only thing that briefly halted his effervescence was the sight of Tommy in a wheelchair. For an instant he was speechless. It was a look Tommy had seen all too often, and one he had come to loathe. It was the moment when someone was taken by surprise and couldn't hide their confusion. Herbert blustered through the awkward moment far faster than most. He righted himself within seconds and his goofy smile returned. Instead of the usual apologies or attempts at sympathy, he blurted out;

"Blast it all Tommy, you are looking jolly good for a man I thought was dead!"

The statement threw Tommy for a moment, then he found his smile.

"You too, old man, you too."

Tommy showed Herbert into the parlour. He was relieved that Herbert made no attempt to aid him with his wheelchair, as so many would; it was always an awkward gesture that made Tommy feel even more of an invalid. He wondered if those people ever considered how he moved around the house when no one else was there? Herbert, however, treated him as if he was walking on two legs.

"I say, how are your parents these days?"

There was a difficult pause.

"Ah," Herbert said, embarrassed.

"It was a Zeppelin bomb in London. Damn unfortunate."

"I should say."

"Clara is well though."

"That would be your little sister?"

"Yes."

"The precocious one, who was always interfering in our plans?"

"That would be Clara," Tommy laughed. "And she still interferes, just in other peoples' plans now, and usually for their benefit."

Herbert strolled to the fire and warmed his hands.

"I confess, I only knew you were still alive because of this magazine," Tommy lifted 'Horrid Crimes' off the table and showed it to Herbert. A grin beamed across the latter's face.

"Fabulous bit of rubbish that," he said. "I love the magazine, have a subscription to it. Most of it is rather torrid, but there is one journalist on their team who specialises in cracking articles on crime detection. He came to interview me when he was in London a few months back writing a follow up piece on Jack the Ripper. You know the sort of thing. Thirty years on do we know anything more about the Ripper? Anyway, he paid me a call. I happened to be working on a forged will case at the time and was in London to give evidence at the Old Bailey."

"It says in the article that you have become an expert in handwriting."

"Yes, though it is really a side-line to my day job. I work for a pharmaceutical company now, coming up with all manner of new products. I also do a lot of safety testing, freelance. It's frightening some of the chemicals they put in beauty and health products these days. I have my own laboratory, so I can do independent testing for companies or individuals."

"That sounds interesting."

"It can be. I had this one case, a while back now. I was asked to test a skin whitening product for a well-to-do lady. She was of a dusky complexion and had used the stuff in an attempt to lighten her skin. The results were horrendous. She will probably be permanently scarred," Herbert shook his head sadly. "I was hardly surprised when I did the tests. The stuff was dreadfully caustic, should never have been allowed near a person's skin. Jolly lucky she didn't get any in her eyes, she would have been blinded. She took the manufacturer to court and the product was withdrawn from sale."

"Makes me rather glad I'm not a woman," Tommy said.

"Don't think male health products are any better, goodness no. My advice is to avoid the lot of them."

Herbert flicked open the cover of 'Horrid Crimes', and it was then he noticed the pile of letters Tommy had conspicuously left on the table nearby. For someone fascinated by handwriting, any glimpsed letter demanded attention. Tommy said casually;

"Clara's latest case, someone writing poison pen letters."

"Does she know who?"

"Not yet, no one seems to have recognised the handwriting, and the letters themselves offer little clue."

"Oh, I wouldn't say that," Herbert used the tip of one finger to drag the letters a little nearer, he nonchalantly glanced over them. "Victorian loops, right slant, yes, I would say this was written by a person who was taught to write around the 1850s or 60s. The penmanship was practiced on a slate first, rather than paper, which is why the pen bites so deep. You need to press more firmly on a slate to write than you do with a pen on paper, a habit once developed that is hard to break. Note the slight hesitations after so many words. This person is used to writing with an old-fashioned nib pen that had to be dipped in ink every so often. Regular use forms the habit of knowing when to re-dip the nib before the ink runs out completely and spoils the flow of the lettering. Even when using a modern pen with an ink reservoir, the habit lingers in little, subtle, pauses of the pen. Here, on the end of this 'e' is a clear one. The pen was lifted unconsciously mid word, so the 'e' does not quite join with the letter beside it as it should."

Herbert peered at the letter more closely. The contents were, for the moment, irrelevant to him. It was the way the words were formed that fascinated him.

"The sharp angles at the tops of some letters, this 'o' for instance, which has almost become a pyramid with a rounded bottom, is taken as a sign of a hard person, who was writing with spite and anger on their mind. The words are grouped very tightly, a sign of internal tension, as is the smallness of the words and the way even downward loops, such as on the 'g', barely drop beneath the writing line. And yet, as the letter progresses, the words expand, the tail loops grow. Yes, the person found the process of writing these letters cathartic. It released the tension within them."

"So we are dealing with an older person filled with anger and bitterness, whose only way of expending that fury is to write nasty letters?" Tommy said.

"A woman, I would suspect, some of the language has a feminine tone and the character of some of the letters suggests a female hand, like this 'p' and this 's'. Women tend to create more flowing curves when writing a letter s, men tend to make the curves sharper. Though, that is more subjective than my other observations."

"Hmm," Tommy mused. "Those are certainly insights I would not have noticed."

"With more time, I could perhaps pick out more. I need to get them under a magnifying glass, perhaps test the ink to suggest a source for it. The paper is good quality. I would imagine the ink will be too."

"I don't think Clara would like the letters leaving the house," Tommy admitted reluctantly. "Some of the contents are quite private and personal."

"Gosh, yes, I just read this one. How ghastly!" Herbert was genuinely appalled. "How can anyone write such things?"

"That I don't know," Tommy shrugged. "Would you like a cream horn? I sent for them especially."

Tommy picked up a plate of cakes from the table and held them out towards Herbert.

"I would indeed, my favourites. You know Tommy, I am jolly glad you rang. I've been feeling rather lonely."

"To be honest, so have I," Tommy sighed. "I mean, I have the girls, so I am hardly alone as such. But I've been lacking in male company since I returned. My own fault though, for a time I just didn't want to see any of my old friends."

"That is understandable," Herbert licked cream off his fingers. "War makes one think in a different way. It is hard to imagine how we used to be so carefree. Some of the things I used to worry about seem so unimportant now."

"I miss the cricket team," It was the first time Tommy had said the words out loud and, as he did, he realised how much he meant them. "I miss the glory days of summer before the war. Sunday afternoon on the cricket ground, batting up, bowling for Brighton. The clunk of leather on wood. I even imagined..."

Tommy stopped himself and laughed.

"What did you imagine?" Herbert asked quietly.

Tommy groaned softly.

"I imagined becoming a professional. Not sure how the parents would have taken it, but I was convinced I was good enough to do it."

Herbert did not respond. A silent lament for lost dreams drifted over the table between them. The cream horns on their plate suddenly seemed sour reminders of long ago times.

"Tommy, there was one thing you taught me all those years ago, a thing that kept me going through my horrid schooldays and later in the trenches," Herbert finally said. "You taught me never to give up because, if you give up, then you'll never know if you were just one day, or even one hour away from achieving what you always wanted. At the time, all I wanted was to survive. Well, I did that, but I saw others who gave up and didn't."

"A goal has to be achievable for it to be worth not giving up on," Tommy answered bitterly.

"It was just a thought," Herbert said. "Look, on Saturday the Salvation Army band is playing a concert to raise funds for injured ex-servicemen. I am going to attend. Would you join me?"

Tommy hesitated, wasn't he an injured ex-serviceman?

"I go for the music, really," Herbert tried to defuse the tension. "I like the jolly stuff. And, well, I..." Herbert blushed. "There is this girl in the Salvation band, she plays the trumpet. Did you ever hear of a girl playing a trumpet? She really is quite good, and I said I would go along and watch her. But, I'm a little bit..."

"Shy, old man?" Tommy interpreted.

"I suppose, yes. She scares the life out of me, to be honest. But I am determined not to give up! Only, a little moral support wouldn't go amiss."

Tommy had to smile. Herbert had not changed a jot since he had last seen him and, as usual, Tommy found it impossible to say no to him.

"All right, you have won me over."

Herbert grinned.

"Thanks for the cake, old man. I must get back. I left an experiment on the boil. You must come to the lab one day."

"Sounds grand."

"I'm jolly pleased you got in touch," Herbert shook Tommy's hand warmly. "You know, that was one of the other things I didn't give up on. I didn't give up on surviving and I didn't give up hoping that you had made it too. And now here we are."

"And here we are," Tommy repeated.

Herbert stood back and smiled, as if finally believing what his eyes told him – that his old friend was real and sitting just before him.

"It was a long war, Tommy, but we made it."

"Some in better shape than others," Tommy answered morbidly.

Herbert slapped him hard on the shoulder.

"You have all your limbs," he said firmly. "That, my friend, is a very good start."

Chapter Sixteen

Clara checked her wristwatch. It was ten minutes past four and there was no sign of Mrs Prinner. Her neighbour had reported seeing her pop out to the shops a half-hour ago with the baby. She had yet to return. Clara perched herself on the garden wall and decided to wait. It was already dark and the road did not have streetlights, except for some very old gas ones which did not appear to work anymore. Clara didn't much like waiting around in someone's garden in the dark, but Mrs Prinner was not going to elude her, of that much she was certain. She was looking forward to a warm fire and a good dinner when she eventually arrived home.

There were footsteps in the darkness. Clara checked her watch using the light from a nearby house window; it was now fifteen minutes past four. The squeak of a wheel gave Clara hope that this was Mrs Prinner returning with the baby, she had no doubt assumed Clara would have given up waiting five minutes ago. The footsteps slowed as they reached the house. Even in the dark, Mrs Prinner could make out the shape of someone sitting on her garden wall. The pram squeaked to a halt.

"Mrs Prinner," Clara couldn't quite make out the woman, but she felt fairly certain it was her. "I do apologise for being early, I had not realised we had changed the appointment to half four."

"Oh," Mrs Prinner was flustered. "I… I was delayed at the shops. I needed some Syrup of Figs for Ivor."

"The baby?"

"No, my eldest. He is five and… and… his grandmother will be bringing him home soon. He stays with her on a Thursday so I can get my housework done."

"Then we best have our chat before Ivor returns," Clara held open the garden gate for the pram and Mrs Prinner reluctantly pushed the baby to the front door.

It was all too apparent she had been attempting to avoid Clara.

"Mrs Prinner, why are you so concerned about speaking to me?"

"I'm not," Mrs Prinner tried to laugh off the suggestion. "I just lost track of time. That is how it is when you have children."

Mrs Prinner fumbled with her house key. Clara peered into the pram at the sleeping baby; a contented, plump thing with rosy red cheeks.

"Anyway, it's not as though I have anything to tell you."

Clara was sorely tempted to call Mrs Prinner out on a barefaced lie, but bit her tongue. The pram was hauled into the house, the bump up the doorstep not disturbing the slumbering infant, and Clara followed. Mrs Prinner made a fuss of turning on the lights and stirring the parlour fire into life, before offering Clara a chair. Clara observed that the room was cluttered with the debris of household chores; an airing horse had been hastily moved back from the fire and was draped with baby's napkins, a pile of clothes stood waiting to be ironed, while a basket by the chair contained a mountain of socks to darn. An old rag had been left forgotten on the mantelpiece from when Mrs Prinner had made a start on the dusting before being distracted, and tucked behind an ornament was a jar of lead black for the fireplace hearth. The room was awash with half-begun tasks, destined never to be fully finished.

Mrs Prinner pulled a teddy-bear from under a cushion and tucked it up with the baby in the pram. She was avoiding meeting Clara's eyes.

"I read the letter you received," Clara said, deciding she would have to force the issue. "Suggesting you had spread lies about a certain Miss Grimes out of jealousy."

"Yes," Mrs Prinner faffed around the baby's pram. "Nonsense, of course."

"Who is Miss Grimes?"

"My cousin," Mrs Prinner shrugged. "I don't see her very often now, but I used to a lot as a child."

"And the rumours?"

Mrs Prinner shook her head.

"I had no need to say anything. People talk about a thing like that. But they blamed me because, well, they said I was jealous. Jealous!" Mrs Prinner snorted. "They should look at themselves for jealousy. Miss Grimes was said to be involved with a married man. That is as much as I knew. I deliberately kept out of it. But people are not blind and they talk. The gossip grew so bad she had to move away. People felt sorry for the wife of the man, naturally."

"The letter against you seemed very personal, more personal than the others."

Mrs Prinner fluffed the baby's blanket and the little creature moaned in its sleep.

"You know who sent the letters, Mrs Prinner," Clara persisted.

"How should I know over everyone else?" The woman laughed. "You've been talking to Mrs Wilton. She imagines she knows people better than they do themselves."

"Maybe she is right, in this instance?"

"I know as much about those letters as any other poor soul who received one. They are despicable and the person who sent them is horrible, but I can't say any more than that."

"Then I am at a dead end," Clara sighed. "I had in mind the Cotterley sisters were behind this."

Mrs Prinner gave a little jerk, enough for Clara to notice and to note it.

"But Miss Wicks seems convinced her letter was by someone else," Clara finished.

Mrs Prinner should have relaxed at this statement, instead she seemed more tense than ever and, at long last, Clara felt she was heading in the right direction.

"Do you know the Cotterley sisters?" Clara asked.

Mrs Prinner took a while to answer.

"They are my great aunts," she said at last.

"Then Miss Grimes is…" Clara was cut off by the front door opening and a child giving a huge bellow of 'hello', before charging down the hallway and straight up to his mother. Ivor had returned.

"I must get on with supper," Mrs Prinner told Clara, her relief at escaping the interview evident. She bustled off Ivor with the excuse of getting him to wash his hands and take off his shoes.

Clara decided she would have to let herself out. In the hallway she came across Mrs Prinner's mother, trying to fold up an old umbrella so she could jam it into the hall stand. The umbrella clearly had other ideas. Clara met her eyes.

"Are you that detective woman?"

"Yes," said Clara.

"Maud Harris," the woman introduced herself.

"Clara Fitzgerald," Clara responded.

"I would talk with you," Maud said, glancing down the hall to where her daughter had vanished into the kitchen. "See you tomorrow, Janice."

From the kitchen came a voice saying goodbye.

"I'll walk with you a bit," Maud nodded to Clara and followed her out the door.

Once on the pavement outside she began to talk.

"What did my daughter tell you?"

"Very little," admitted Clara.

"She thinks her great aunts are behind all this."

"The Cotterley sisters?"

"Yes, well, they are called that, but Heather Cotterley was married to Martin Jenkins. She only reverted to her maiden name when he died."

"And, are you related to them?"

"Heavens, no! Or at least not by blood, only marriage," Maud laughed grimly. "Mighty relieved I am about that too. There is madness in the women of that family. I worry about Janice a little because of it. No, my husband's father was a Cotterley. But, you see, he died in an accident when my husband was quite little, and my mother-in-law remarried to a Mr Harris and changed her son's surname. That did not go down well with the Cotterleys, no indeed!"

"Do you think they are behind these letters?"

"Almost certainly," Maud nodded, "I don't know why, nor how you will prove it. But the handwriting looks like that of Heather Cotterley."

"You recognised it?"

"To a degree. We used to get Christmas cards until they shut themselves away from the world. I suppose it is five years since I last had any form of communication with them."

"And I don't suppose you kept any of these cards."

"No," Maud shrugged. "Why would I? They are the sort of people you avoid if you can. I don't know what turned them so bitter, well, sometimes I think I do. I imagine Heather being widowed young made them angry. They are the sort of people who think the world owes them something and that they are the only people to ever have a grave misfortune befall them. Heather's husband died in the same accident as their brother. The two men were out on a barge with a lot of other people for a pleasure trip. The barge capsized. Officially it was said there had been too many people on board. I hear tell the Cotterleys went into such a fury people thought they had gone insane. They raged at the company who rented out the barge, at the poor souls who survived the calamity, even the vicar who took the funeral! They screamed at him that they would never forgive God for taking their menfolk. Oh, it was quite the drama."

"Did Heather have a daughter?"

"Yes, Yvetta. Poor girl was always under her mother's tyranny. First chance she got she married."

"Would that be to a Mr Grimes?"

"Thomas Grimes, yes. He's a butcher and a very nice fellow. But he won't have anything to do with his mother-in-law or her sisters. Did Janice tell you about Miss Grimes?"

"Yes."

"Takes after her grandmother, that one," Maud shook her head sadly. "You see, Yvetta would let her daughter, Ellen, visit the Cotterleys all the time, and they skewed her thinking with all manner of fancies. I dare say they encouraged her little fling too. The man had a bit of money, and the Cotterleys only ever think of money, you aren't anyone if you haven't a few shillings in your pocket. Yvetta married beneath herself, or so they felt. They wanted more for little Ellen. So she got in with this gentleman who was having troubles at home. I think they believed his tall tales about getting a divorce and marrying the girl. This was during the war and he was an officer in the army too. Their heads were quite turned."

"But he didn't divorce his wife?"

"Oh, he did, eventually. But he never married Ellen Grimes. No, he found some pretty girl with air for brains and a good inheritance. I hear tell he moved to the South of France with her and wastes his time and her money in the sun all day. You see, he never had the money the Cotterleys imagined, it was all façade. Little Ellen was disgraced and moved away. That must be over two years ago now."

"What was the name of the married man?"

"He was a Major in the army. Let me think. Yes, he

was Major Dennis."

"Does his former wife still live around here?"

"I believe so, everyone was very kind to her, you see. And she did better out of the divorce than Major Dennis banked on. Her name was Eva Dennis, but she must have reverted to her maiden name now, which I don't remember."

"I imagine all this turmoil upset the Cotterley sisters deeply."

"Oh yes, and they attacked my daughter for it!" Maud clenched her fists angrily. "My Janice kept well out of it, but they blamed her anyway. Said she had spread lies about Ellen because she was jealous of her being courted by a Major, and if she had not done so, then Ellen would not have had to move away. I never heard such rot! As if Ellen's activities had not been noticed by others. My Janice married a good man. He's a plumber and keeps a sound roof over their heads. But the Cotterleys think he is worthless because he doesn't work in an office. They assume Janice must be unhappy because her husband is a workman. As I say, they are all about money and snobbery."

They had come to the corner of the road. Maud stopped and indicated she was to head right, while Clara was headed left.

"Thank you for the information, Mrs Harris. Should I have any more questions, might I call on you?"

"Of course. I have no qualms talking about them. Janice is so worried they will cause her more trouble, so she won't say anything."

"I can understand that."

"Well, I say they need reminding they can't go around treating people like dirt."

Clara said farewell and they parted company. As she walked on into the dark night, she found her thoughts returning to Constable Brompton. She wondered how he was. It was probably too soon to pay him a call, but it was tempting, nonetheless. She resisted the urge. She should get home and have some dinner, warm herself, and prepare for tomorrow. She was certain she was on to something with the Cotterley sisters, but pinning them down was going to be a challenge and, until she did, they were free to spread their venom. So far no one had come to harm because of it, but if the letters continued she could not be certain that would last. She mused on the strangeness of people all the way home.

Chapter Seventeen

When Clara rose the next morning, the post had already arrived. She picked it up from the door mat and joined Tommy in the parlour, where he was devouring a plate of toast. Clara used a knife from the table to slit open the letter. She already recognised the handwriting on the envelope and knew what to expect;

Dear Miss Fitzgerald,

We find ourselves wondering what sort of woman takes delight in interfering in other peoples' business? We have come to the conclusion you are a busybody and a gossip. Interfering in other people's lives is wickedness! Instead of prying into the business of others, you would make better use of your time finding a husband, before you are too old to be a bride. You are already past the first blush of youth, wait any longer and no man will show the slightest interest in you. As for this detective lark, it is really disgraceful, and the sign of a woman of low moral fibre. We only state this in the hope you might improve yourself.

Clara laughed.

"Talk about the kettle calling the pot black!" she showed the letter to Tommy, who took it with far less complacency.

"Who do they think they are?" he snapped.

"Oh, I expected it," Clara smiled. "I would have been disappointed had they not sent me one. I do rather feel it is lacking the gusto of the others. But, then again, I suppose they know only a very little about me."

Clara took some toast and examined the next letter on the table. The handwriting on this one was not familiar, but it was locally posted. Clara slipped the knife into the envelope and opened it.

"Ah, good! It is a letter from Colonel Fairbanks asking me to call on him sometime today," Clara took note of the address. "Goodness, if I am to get to him and be back in time for my appointment with Mr Johnson I really shall have to dash. I am going to have to invest in a bicycle."

Tommy raised his eyes and looked dubious.

"I remember the last time you were on a bicycle."

"You get better with practice," Clara said confidently. "Well done on finding Herbert, by the way, not just for his expertise, it's nice that you two can catch up. You were good friends."

"We were," Tommy agreed. "I hope we still are. Chalk and cheese we might be, but somehow we rub along well."

"Did he really call me interfering?" Clara asked after a moment.

"And precocious."

Clara gave a decisive nod.

"I shall take it all as a compliment. Take care, see you at teatime," with that she was out the door and heading for the outskirts of town yet again.

~~~ * ~~~

Colonel Fairbanks had retired to Brighton after a lifetime of living in a city. The clean air (so the doctors had assured him), would do his lungs the world of good, and the fresh, clean waters (if he would only partake in them), would work wonders on his grumpy digestive system. Fairbanks had heeded certain portions of the advice, and had bought a nice villa-style house at the very edge of town. He had good views of the countryside all around him, and plenty of fresh air. But he took exception to bathing in seawater, or (Heaven forbid!) actually drinking it, and had not even taken a stroll on Brighton's famous beaches since his arrival. He was much more content to sit in his garden, smoking a large pipe full of the filthiest tobacco, and imagining himself away to the dingy streets of London and the crimes he had once been summoned to solve.

He was a man who was bored. Bored by the peace and quiet. Bored by the inactivity. Bored by rounds at the golf course or lunch at his club. Bored, bored, bored! Retirement, Fairbanks finally concluded after a year of tedium, was all right for some, but not a man like himself, who loved the thrill of adventure and the drama of a good hunt. But there was nothing else for it. A man doesn't leave the Force then ask for his job back. A man must lie in the bed he makes for himself, and so Fairbanks was making the best of things.

His letter all those months back to the Gazette, had been written on one of his dark days, when he was sick and tired of doing nothing. Constable Brompton's accident had struck him as suspicious but, with no way back into the Force (lest he be called an interfering old policeman who should leave the real work to younger men) his only option was to write a letter to the paper, and hope to attract attention. At the time it had failed. No one was interested in the ramblings of an old man. He had let the matter drop, however much his old detective's nose hated to do so, and went back to learning how to grow roses. It seemed the thing to do when one was retired.

Clara's letter had, therefore, taken him by surprise. He was delighted that at last someone was taking him seriously and wrote back to her at once. Her arrival at his home that morning only added to his good humour. She had arrived in good time for a leisurely brunch (something the Colonel had developed a habit for when his working hours had often seen him out before the crack of dawn) and he explained the concept of his mid-morning indulgence as he led her through to a warm parlour.

"Brunch, is the meal between breakfast and, as the Americans call it, lunch. I supposed it is rather the morning equivalent of supper. I always insist on crumpets and bacon rolls. Followed by a substantial walk around the neighbourhood. One must always pay for one's sins with hard work," The Colonel patted his stomach which, while by no means the svelte belly of his youth, remained trim despite his gargantuan appetite. "When one is retired, one has a lot of time for walking."

The Colonel almost sighed mournfully, then remembered he had a guest present. Fairbanks held to the principle that one never showed unhappiness before a stranger.

"I assume you came to the police after a spell in the army?" Clara asked as they settled before a comforting fire and awaited the arrival of brunch.

"Slightly more complicated than that," Colonel Fairbanks smiled. "I entered the police in 1868, just as a constable. They were very different days then. I lost my patience with the job, and left to join the army. I had some money behind me, from my late uncle, and was able to buy a commission. Two decades later and I was a Colonel with a touch of malaria that made continued campaigning out in foreign climes rather unpalatable. I spoke to a few friends in high places, and was side-stepped into the police force as a Chief Inspector. It was the role I had always wanted. For the next twenty years I plumbed the depths of London's criminal underworld, solving everything from petty theft to murder. Then they suggested I retire and make way for a younger man," Fairbanks shrugged his broad shoulders. "Experience, it appears, counts for very little when age is a consideration."

"You miss policing?"

"I can't deny it. I have a mind for puzzles, always have."

The crumpets and bacon rolls arrived. The Colonel took a toasting fork from the fireplace and impaled a soft crumpet on the end, before propping it before the fire. Meanwhile he offered Clara a roll.

"And you Miss Fitzgerald? What brings you to this business?"

"I suppose a mixture of curiosity, nosiness and a desire to help people," Clara replied.

Colonel Fairbanks liked the answer.

"And you are looking into the matter of Constable Brompton's accident?"

"I have been asked to make discreet enquiries, yes. Which is why your letter intrigued me."

The Colonel nodded.

"I still believe what I stated last summer. There was something wrong about that incident."

"I concur, but perhaps you will explain your reasons for thinking that, and what you know of the matter?"

Colonel Fairbanks retrieved the toasted crumpet and dropped it onto a plate for Clara, before starting another. He was delighted to at last have an audience for his suspicions.

"I am no Sherlock Holmes," he began. "But I found, from just the little I read in the papers, that the case made no sense as an accident. Let's begin with the lane Constable Brompton was traversing, now, I went and took a look, and it is not the sort of track any driver would negotiate at speed without good reason. It bends and twists, have you seen it?"

"Yes, and it didn't strike me as a good road to drive fast down."

"And at night, too," Fairbanks talked with his hands, his forgotten crumpet burning in the fire. "But, by some stroke of good fortune for our driver, or so it would seem, he happened to come across Constable Brompton on the one spot where the road briefly becomes straight and allows the driver a chance to accelerate. Coincidence or design? Now, the driver didn't stop, but that is not entirely uncommon. Reckless drivers also tend to be the least concerned by the consequences of their actions. However, the car must have been badly damaged. The force of the impact alone should have dented the bonnet, not to mention it must have caused the car to veer, possibly hitting one of the stone walls that edges the lane. When I went to the spot just a couple of weeks after the incident I spotted red paint on the stone wall. I would suggest that our car was red and collided with that wall before driving off."

"A red car with considerable damage to the front end should be reasonably easy to find, you would imagine," Clara said.

"Clearly you have had the same thought as me, Miss Fitzgerald – where is the car? If it belonged to someone local, or even a visitor to the area, you would have thought someone would have noticed it. The car would have needed to be taken straight to a garage, yet, from the enquiries I have made, no mechanic has tended to such a car. It seems to have just vanished."

"Highly suspicious."

"Yes. Of course, we might argue the person was fearful they would be identified by the damage to the car, and drove to a distant garage, but I suspect the vehicle would have been in rather a poor condition to drive. Even if the impact made by Brompton had not damaged something mechanical, the collision with the wall certainly would have. It almost seems as if the person driving the car was able to make it disappear. Perhaps into a barn or something similar? Somewhere it could be hidden while it was fixed and perhaps the paint colour changed."

"As far as I am aware, there is no one in Brighton who owns such a car," Clara said carefully. "And a visitor would not have access to a hiding spot on such short notice."

"Unless they had planned to run down Constable Brompton, and had made suitable advance arrangements."

Clara thought about this for a moment. Her

conversation with Farmer White had convinced her all the more that Brompton's misfortune was more than just an accident, but so far she had no hard evidence to back up her suspicions.

"I mulled the matter over with the fellows at my club," Fairbanks continued. "According to them, there are ten households in the vicinity of the town that own cars. Two of which are red. One happens to belong to a golfing chum, and I see his car every week when I go to play a round. It is in pristine condition, not a scrape or a bump, and, if I am honest, the owner is not the sort to drive above 10mph at his worst. The second belongs to a woman, a little sporty thing, the car, that is. When I made further enquiries I found it had suffered a problem with the engine at the time of the accident and had been waiting to be fixed for nearly a month. She, or anyone else, could not have driven it that night."

"So we must assume the car was not local."

"Yes, which makes it even stranger that it just disappeared with no one seeing it. Someone, you would imagine, would see a badly damaged red car leaving the area of Brighton. They would have had to stop for petrol, at least."

"It could be they travelled at night and were lucky," Clara said, deciding to air out all possibilities.

"There is one other thing," Fairbanks paused as the smell of burning crumpet reached his nose. He pulled the toasting fork out of the fire with a mild curse and removed the blackened crumpet, tossing it onto the hearth stone. As he began toasting another he continued. "When I was in London, we saw a number of cases just like this, we called them 'hits and runs'. They became extremely popular among the criminal fraternity as a means of getting rid of someone."

"Really?" Clara was intrigued.

"You see, if you stab or shoot a man, it is very difficult to convince anyone it was an accident. But run a man over with a car and, if you are caught, you can say to a judge that you never saw the fellow in the dark, or he just stepped off the pavement in front of you. It is much harder to prove it wasn't an accident. And it can mean the difference between a prison sentence and the hangman's noose."

"Yet there still remains the question, why?" Clara retrieved the crumpet from the fire herself this time, before it burned. The Colonel thanked her with an abashed smile.

"Miss Fitzgerald, can you provide any insight into why someone would wish to harm Brompton?"

Clara drew in a breath – could she?

"Brompton seems to remember very little about his life before the accident. It is possible he stumbled across something he shouldn't have," Clara refrained from suggesting police corruption, though she had no doubt the shrewd Colonel had already suspected as much.

"I might be reading too much into this whole affair," Colonel Fairbanks admitted, buttering his slightly singed crumpet. "But the majority of road accidents are very clear-cut. You know who must have been behind it almost at once. To me, this whole thing reeks of organised crime."

"Organised crime?" Clara was surprised. "Can there be such a thing?"

"Oh yes, I'm afraid the police have been rather slowly catching up with the notion. We have always known about criminal gangs, of course, but organised crime is something much bigger. It is like a business, but being run outside of the law. There is a structure to it, and there are those within it who never get their hands dirty. In fact, in some cases, the head of the operation is not even in this country. We thought at first it was an Italian specialty, how naïve of us! I'm afraid everyone is involved, the Chinese, the Russians, the Irish, the Jews. Naturally it works best in London, but often these organisations have a far reach, and the police are always one step behind. Like the mythical hydra, we cut off one head and two more appear. It is the scourge of modern policing and, as far as I can see, we are making little impact on it."

"That is disturbing," Clara found the whole idea of crime being run like a business disconcerting. "I hate to think of it happening in Brighton, yet, I can see why it might. Brighton attracts the criminal element with its racing and gambling. There is big money to be made here."

"Yes. And the ease with which a criminal from London can travel here by train makes it all the more tempting."

Clara didn't like such ideas, but they fitted in with Inspector Park-Coombs notion that he had a corrupt policeman in his midst, and then there was all that business with Billy 'Razor' Brown; he had his dirty fingers in many criminal pies, she was sure of it.

"Miss Fitzgerald, the key to this is Constable Brompton. As long as he poses no threat, he will probably be left alone, but if he remembers something and his assailant finds out..." Fairbanks left the sentence hanging. He didn't need to list the possible things that might be done to Brompton to silence him.

Clara suddenly felt a pang of anxiety. Someone had attacked Brompton at the police station because they believed he had remembered something, but they had been disturbed before they could kill him. Now he was alone in the hospital, would they resist the temptation to finish the job? Could they risk it? Her mind flashed back to stumbling into the corridor straight on top of Alfie Ling. Where could he have appeared from except the far door of the archives room? Clara felt a little sick and suddenly the bacon rolls turned her stomach.

"Thank you for the brunch, Colonel Fairbanks. You have given me an idea I must act on at once," Clara rose. She was thinking she must get back to the hospital immediately and check on Brompton.

"Do call again if I can be of any help," Fairbanks said, trying to hide the hint of desperation from his voice. He had enjoyed mulling over a criminal matter more than he cared to admit to himself.

Clara hurried out of the Colonel's villa and started at a brisk trot for home. Her mind was whirring with possibilities, but one thing was certain – she had to tell Park-Coombs about Alfie Ling as soon as possible and have someone reliable keep a watch over Brompton while he recovered. She suddenly felt a pang of anger with the young constable – why had he walked back into a hornet's nest alone? Had he confided in her, then at least she wouldn't be groping in the dark, and he would not be lying unconscious on a hospital bed with a bump on his head. Then again, perhaps he had not trusted her enough? She had not really given much information about herself or her role during their conversation. Oh, but if he had only spoken with the Inspector!

It was no time to be angry. Clara reached a crossroads and found herself glancing up and down for a red car. Then she hurried across, hoping she was not too late.

Chapter Eighteen

It was almost midday when Clara reached the hospital. Her feet were killing her, and she had only a short while before she must hasten to her appointment with Mr Johnson, but she could not tame her anxiety enough to resist checking on Brompton. Naturally, it was not visiting time and the woman on the reception desk treated Clara with well-practiced disdain.

"You will have to come back at two o'clock," she informed her in a crisp tone.

"I merely want to know how Constable Brompton is doing," Clara insisted. "I can't come back at two."

"That is hardly my concern."

Clara felt like screaming. Why were people so impossible?

"Has he woken up at all?"

"Young lady, I do not know the condition of every patient within this hospital. If you return at visiting time, the ward sister may be able to answer your questions."

Clara wanted to say something, but it was impossible. How could you argue with a woman who had bureaucracy on her side? Clara tried to think of a good argument to win her over, then gave in and retreated outside. She stood in the cold wind, thinking. Finally she went back inside and asked to use a telephone. This created more argument, as the only 'phone was in the office behind the woman and she wasn't keen to let Clara near it. But Clara was not going to let the idea drop. It was only when people started to look over curiously at the argumentative young woman, that the receptionist gave in and showed Clara to the office. She hovered over her, while Clara made her call.

"May I speak to Inspector Park-Coombs, please?" Clara said into the receiver, thinking that he might have the authority to give her access to Constable Brompton.

She was to be disappointed. The Desk Sergeant informed her that the Inspector was out on police business and was not expected back for some time. Clara was just putting down the 'phone, trying not to look directly in the eye of the irate receptionist, when she caught a glimpse of someone over the woman's shoulder.

"That man," she pointed, "is he allowed to go up to the wards?"

The receptionist swung around, her stout form seeming to swivel like a gargantuan marble statue on a pedestal.

"No." she said in a voice of thwarted authority. "He is not!"

She was starting to head out of the office, but Clara skipped past her. She had recognised the man at once, despite him being out of uniform. She had Alfie Ling's face and appearance burned into her memory. The receptionist squawked as Clara ducked around the front desk and dashed to the staircase in hot pursuit of Ling.

"You can't go up outside of visiting hours!" the woman wailed.

"He did!" Clara pointed out, no longer caring about the woman's outrage. She was worried about Brompton, and what Ling intended to do when he reached him.

The receptionist was still protesting as Clara hurried up the stairs. No doubt a hospital porter would be summoned soon and sent to catch the ill-mannered visitors who had disobeyed the commands of the receptionist. In the meantime, she wanted to make sure Ling could cause no harm to Brompton. The problem was she had no idea which floor Brompton was on, and there happened to be three. Clara came to the first landing and peered through the double doors that led onto a corridor. There was no sign of Ling. She ran up to the next floor, regretting her footwear choice once again. She would have to invest in a pair of those ghastly walking boots she had seen advertised in a magazine. They would look absurd with a dress, but at least she would be able to continue her detecting without being in agony all the time.

On the second floor, the double doors were just swinging closed. She pushed them open and entered a corridor. On her left were a series of long open wards filled with men who, where able, glanced up at her as she entered. On her right were several private rooms for seriously ill or contagious patients, and just ahead was the broad back of Alfie Ling, standing at the door of one of the rooms.

Clara ran forwards, not entirely certain what she was going to do once she reached the man, but certain that she must do something.

"Constable!" she called.

As she had suspected, addressing him by his official title caused Alfie to look up faster than had she just called his name. It was the natural, instinctive reaction of a man who spends most of his time patrolling roads and being summoned by concerned passers-by. Clara ran to him and put a hand on his arm.

"What are you doing here?" she asked, in-between catching her breath.

"I've come to see Constable Brompton," Alfie Ling peered at her for a moment. "Oh, it's you, Miss Fitzgerald. I didn't recognise you, with you being all red in the face like that."

"Running up two flights of concrete steps in high heels

will do that to a woman," Clara replied. "I have to ask, what is that in your coat pocket?"

Ling had his hand in his coat pocket, apparently holding something. He looked at it sheepishly.

"Can't say."

"Constable Ling, if you don't tell me, I shall be forced to summon Inspector Park-Coombs and tell him that I suspect you of attempting to harm Constable Brompton!"

Ling's mouth dropped open with honest surprise. His previously mild expression soured, and the corners of his mouth dropped down. A sudden anger filled Alfie Ling and when he spoke it was through clenched teeth.

"That is an awful thing to accuse a man of. Especially when you are talking about his closest friend. Here, if you must see it!" Ling drew his hand from his pocket and revealed two packets of cigarettes. "They don't allow a man his fags in here."

Clara stared at the cardboard boxes in his hand. Innocuous things compared to the lump of stone or piece of brick she had feared. The shape they had formed in his pocket had looked like something hard Ling could use to finish off the job he began at the police station. Now she found herself doubting her own observations. Not that a badly injured man needed much help dying. A pillow over the face would be sufficient. Clara pursed her lips, a frown of uncertainty on her face.

"You were in the basement when Brompton was attacked."

"Yes," Ling nodded his head vigorously. "Who do you think got him down there when he asked to see the archives again? But I didn't hurt him. I let him into the archives and went to check on the boiler. We had no heat, except from the coal fires, and everyone was complaining. I was just coming back when you burst out of the archives."

Ling's expression changed again, to one of dawning realisation.

"How do I know you didn't hit him over the head, and

then pretended to run for help?"

Clara was appalled at the suggestion.

"I had no motive to do such a thing!"

"Nor did I!"

They were glowering at each other when a porter suddenly appeared and yelled at them. Ling looked abashed at having snuck in, admitting to the porter he had chanced his arm, since he was on duty during normal visiting hours. Clara maintained a stance of righteous rule-breaking; she had disobeyed official instructions through fear a man was to be harmed. The porter was not impressed by either explanation and shuffled them both out of the hospital. The receptionist smirked at them as they were chucked out the doors.

A thin rain was falling as they stood on the steps of the hospital indignantly.

"How could you think I hurt Brompton?" Alfie Ling was still smarting from the accusation. "Brompton is the only decent friend I have in this world."

"The circumstances were suspicious," Clara found herself apologising. "And it had to be a policeman behind the attack."

"Or you."

Clara chose to ignore that.

"James Brompton helped me when no one else would," Alfie Ling continued, cold rain plastering his hair to his forehead. "He saved me from a life of crime and ruin. I owe him everything and I would never hurt him. I came here today to make sure he was safe, and to see if he could tell me anything about who attacked him. I'm not stupid Miss Fitzgerald, I know this was an inside job, and I now start to believe what Brompton told me about the night he was knocked down by that car."

"He told you about that?"

"Yes. He didn't trust anyone else. He was certain it was because he had come across some information by accident that he was struck down. Someone wanted him killed before he could expose them, and that someone was a policeman," Ling suddenly looked incredibly sad. "I joined the Force because I wanted to be removed from the scumbags and the dregs of society I was born among. I wanted to work in a world maintained by order and honesty. Instead, I find there are scumbags in uniforms, just as there are scumbags in rags."

Clara found herself watching the man's face. His emotions danced across his features as openly and unrestrained as a young child's. If Alfie Ling was acting the part, he was certainly a proficient performer, one the silent movie makers would love to have in their studios. Clara somehow felt Ling didn't have the subtlety to be that cunning. She found herself believing him, which meant she was now without a suspect for the attack on Brompton.

"Constable Ling, might I suggest we retreat to a teashop and have a conversation about this matter? I have a feeling that you and I are on the same side, which means we may be able to help each other."

Ling considered the offer. The rain was beating down on them both, and he was soaked through already. He wasn't sure what to make of Clara. He knew her reputation, naturally, but he did not know if she could be trusted. This matter of Brompton had left him feeling wary of everyone. On the other hand, Ling was desperate to talk to someone, and it would be better if that person was as far removed from the police force as possible, without being so removed that they could not understand the seriousness of the matter. He considered a moment longer, then agreed. They walked to the nearest teashop and found a cosy seat near a fireplace so they could dry out a little. Clara ordered sandwiches for them both, and carefully unpinned her sodden hat, propping it by the fire. It would no doubt lose its shape, just like the last one she had been wearing when she was caught in the rain. It was becoming rather a bad habit.

"Now Constable Ling, where shall we begin?"

"I want to know why you are interested in Brompton,"

Ling said cautiously. "I don't really trust you."

He said the last sentence in an apologetic tone and without meeting her eyes.

"On that score, we find ourselves in similar positions," Clara said sadly. "I can't be certain I trust you either. Circumstances make me hesitant. Perhaps you might elaborate on your relationship with Brompton?"

Ling gave this some thought, but it was obvious to them both that this was not a compromising matter. Anyone within the police force could tell Clara of the friendship between Ling and Brompton, had Clara only asked.

"Brompton got me into the police. It wasn't an easy matter, either. I had a reputation locally, nothing on record, fortunately, but everyone knew…" Alfie Ling sighed. "That maid of yours, Annie, she took one look at me that day I came to your house last year and I saw in her eyes what she thought of me. A criminal in a uniform, that is all a lot of people see, even you."

Clara started to deny this, but bit her tongue, she had viewed Ling as a wolf in sheep's clothing; it had been obvious on her face from the start.

"Well, I am not a criminal, not anymore. Oh, I was a bad lad, sure enough. I made all sorts of trouble, mostly because I knew no better and because I hated everyone. You see, I loved my mother, but I knew others looked down on her. When you are boy, you don't understand that, and it grows into resentment. My mother was a tart, probably still is, though I haven't seen her in years. I have no idea who my father was, probably she doesn't either. She used to call all her man friends 'uncle this' or 'uncle that' and a small child gives it no thought. But the older I became, the more I understood. People looked at my mother like she was filth. She didn't seem to care, or maybe she didn't notice. She had a drinking problem, which later became a cocaine problem. I don't suppose half the time she knew much who she was, let alone what other people were thinking.

"She tried to look after me at first. She would buy food and leave it in a cupboard. If I was hungry I had to find something in there. I had to learn to cook young, mother hardly ever did, and you can't eat raw potatoes. I tried it once and was so ill mother had to call a doctor, one of her friends I think. He gave her a stern lecture on responsibilities, which was rather rich, but she did improve for a bit. She taught me how to boil potatoes and eggs, and to make a thin porridge from oats and breadcrumbs. I lived on that for years.

"She was a kind woman, but off her head most of the time. I drifted about. No one saw the need to send me to school. Only when a truancy officer appeared at the house one day did it even occur to my mother that a child needed educating. I was seven when I stepped into a classroom, and I hated it. I worried about my mother all the time, I didn't like her being alone, and I was so far behind the other children. I only stuck at it because mother cried when the truancy officer called again, and begged me to be a good boy and go to school every day, and learn to read and write, so I wouldn't end up like her."

Alfie Ling paused, his lips had tightened into a narrow line. Once again Clara saw how Ling's emotions played across his face with no attempt to mask them. He would make an awful gambler and an even worse criminal. His was not a face that could lie.

Ling broke from his reverie slowly.

"I used to feel angry a lot. I can't say why, it became such a common emotion for me that I stopped noticing it. It was just part of my normal self. I detested all my mother's neighbours. I had this strange idea that if they wanted to they could help her. Now I realise she was beyond help. In any case, I don't think she wanted to change. As I grew older I used to cause trouble, I would lash out, and for a moment I would feel better. Then I would be punished and the anger was ten times worse. Had I carried on like that I would, no doubt, be rotting in some prison somewhere. But mother became sick – I'm not sure what it was. With wiser eyes on me now, I wonder if she was expecting another child. In any case, I was sent to live with some aunt I had never even heard of. I was twelve and I caused the sort of chaos to that poor woman that only a feral, wrathful child can. I imagine it would have ended in the workhouse or something similar, had not I met James Brompton.

"This aunt, whoever she really was, lived in a cottage that was part of a farm estate. She made lace for a living, and the estate owner allowed her to live in the cottage free of rent because she was the widow of a stockman who had served the farmer for five decades. Anyway, at the time James' grandparents lived nearby, and he came to visit them every weekend. One day we simply met. He was standing on a bridge staring at a stream. I was just wandering about as I did, and he asked me if I knew how to catch fish. I said I didn't and he said he didn't either, and that was how it began. I lived for the weekends after that. James taught me everything he knew about the countryside. We would collect bird eggs, or hunt for badger setts. He did learn how to fish eventually and he taught me. Whenever I found myself in trouble, James would ask me why I had done such a bad thing, and more often than not I couldn't answer. Somehow, being unable to explain myself to James made me embarrassed, and it also made me stop and wonder, why had I done bad things? When you can't explain things to yourself you feel a fool. So I stopped doing bad things. Besides, it was more fun learning all the stuff James knew.

"It helped that I was in a different place, around people who didn't know much about my past. I made friends with some of the farm labourers and they even gave me some work tending the animals. For around five years I was happier than I had ever been before. Then the war came. James was eager to sign up, we were both old enough. I wasn't so sure. The farm was nice and I had never thought about killing anyone. Odd thing to say, I suppose, when most people back home considered me a young thug. But really, the thought of guns and fighting scared me.

"James went without me. He served a full two years before someone realised he was more valuable out of the trenches working on maps and intelligence. He was involved in the background of quite a few famous campaigns. But he came home without a fanfare or a medal, except the standard ones everyone got, even though he deserved a lot more. His work was rather hush-hush."

"It sounds as though James Brompton was a very clever man." Clara said, somewhat surprised.

"Oh he still is, don't doubt that. But, you see, the sort of work he did during the war, well, there isn't much call for that in the civilian world. James fancied doing something different when he got home. He thought he would make a fine detective, but there was no call for extra detectives in Brighton, so he took a job as a constable, to fit himself in and learn about opportunities. That was around the time of the police strikes and, when the trouble died down, James told me I could earn more with the police now there had been all the commotion, than I did on the farm. Also, it would give me prospects. There weren't really many prospects in farm labouring, I had seen that. So I didn't think I could lose, and here I am."

"What about your mother?" Clara asked curiously. "What became of her?"

Ling shrugged.

"She never wrote to say I could come home. I probably wouldn't have gone anyway. She probably just forgot about me, or maybe she thought she had written the letter when she really hadn't. She was like that. Forgetting things all the time."

Clara nodded. She felt she was beginning to understand Alfie Ling. She was also beginning to trust him. His story was so complex and detailed that it seemed impossible that it was a complete lie. It also made a lot of sense, how else could Alfie Ling – the troubled little boy – end up in the police?

"Now it is your turn, Miss Fitzgerald, what is your interest in Brompton?" Ling spoke quietly, but it was plain he expected an answer. After the story he had given her, Clara decided it was only fair she was honest too.

"I think Constable Brompton is the victim of police corruption, stemming back to his accident last summer. Someone within the Brighton police is crooked. I have suspected as much since last year when Billy 'Razor' Brown made his escape from your police cells," Clara discreetly kept the Inspector's name out of the conversation. She was still inclined to be wary.

"I have come to the same conclusion," Ling replied. "That car accident didn't feel right. I searched high and low for the vehicle involved, I should have been able to find it, but I couldn't. And now this? James said he wanted to check some information in the archives, I think he was looking for a clue to who had tried to kill him."

"But, when I talked to Brompton, he seemed to remember nothing about the accident?" Clara was remembering the young man with the vague eyes and no short term memory, who had sat before her only a few days ago.

"I wouldn't care to contradict you," Ling said carefully. "But James Brompton is far cleverer than anyone else I know alive. He stumbled on something, something dangerous. I said he was clever, but he doesn't have much common sense. I intend to keep an eye on him and, if I can, find out who hurt him. And Heaven help 'em when I do."

"You have no idea who did this?"

"No, but I would sorely like to find out."

A darkness came over Ling's face, and Clara saw a man who would act impulsively and dangerously to protect his friend. She also recognised a man who didn't trust anybody.

"Constable Ling, I want exactly the same. If you can see your way to helping me, then maybe we can resolve this conspiracy?"

Ling studied her face for a long time. His own was a blank mask. He didn't know what to think or how to act for the best, but he did know that alone he would not be able to solve the mystery.

"I have a vested interest in this too," Clara continued. "Someone helped Razor Brown to escape so that he could come after me. He would have hurt me, maybe killed me, had I not been prepared for him. I want to know who was behind his escape and who put my life in jeopardy. I can hardly work with the police in the future knowing that one, or maybe more, among them is a crook. How can I trust the police after what happened?"

"I see your point," Ling agreed. "I feel the same. I don't know who I can talk to among my colleagues. I feel so alone. I don't even know who James suspected, he has never told me. He said it would only put me in danger too."

"What about the archives he was looking at the day he was attacked?"

"The box was from 'C' section. I looked at it after James was taken to hospital. There was nothing missing, as far as I could see."

"The policeman behind the attack might be intelligent enough to realise that a missing file would only raise more suspicion. I really need to speak to Brompton."

"He is pretty out of it at the moment," Ling looked grim. "I think they shook his brain up pretty good this time."

"Ling, if you can find your way to trusting me, then together I think we can solve this riddle and unmask the man behind this crime."

Ling met her eyes, his own filled with deep sadness.

"I wish I had your confidence."

"It is not about confidence, it is about being jolly good detectives."

Clara paid for their sandwiches and tea, and they went out into the drizzle again. Ling checked his watch and noted it was nearly time for him to go on duty.

"Can I call on you if I find anything out?" he asked. "And you will let me know if you discover anything?"

Clara was glad to hear he was prepared to trust her.

"That would be fine, Constable Ling. Would you mind if I paid a call on Constable Brompton when it is visiting time at the hospital?"

"No. Actually I would be glad if you did. I would like to know someone was keeping an eye on him."

They said their farewells. Clara headed to her next appointment, pushing thoughts of corrupt policemen and vanishing cars from her mind as she went to investigate her other case. There was still a poison pen letter writer to be found.

Chapter Nineteen

Mr Johnson's house was a middle terrace. The blinds were partially closed when Clara arrived. She was five minutes late for her appointment with him and she hoped he would not hold it against her. She rapped the large knocker on the door. No one answered. Clara stomped her cold feet on the doorstep and rapped the knocker again.

"Good afternoon, Miss Fitzgerald."

Clara turned and spotted Matthew O'Donaghue leaning on the garden gate. He doffed his cap to her.

"Mr O'Donaghue," Clara nodded politely, before turning back to the door and rapping the knocker for a third time.

"After Mr Johnson, are you? He should be in. I saw him coming home a good hour ago. I am painting the gate at No.31, you see, and it is dead opposite," O'Donaghue pointed across the road to a house with a partially painted gate. "Is he expecting you?"

"Yes," Clara was beginning to feel concerned. She stepped off the doorstep and peered through the almost closed blinds. Could something have happened to Mr Johnson? Might he have been taken ill? "Does Mr Johnson often miss arranged appointments?"

"No, a very punctual man he is. Never known him miss

a meeting. He is in business, you see, and very professional about it too."

Clara was trying to see into the dim room, but could only catch glimpses. There was the fireplace, unlit, which was odd on such a cold day, and an easy chair set at an angle. She spotted a straggly plant up one corner and the back of a wooden chair. She stepped to the side to get a different angle and found herself catching her breath.

"Good heavens!" Clara stepped back from the window. "Mr O'Donaghue, we must get in at once!"

O'Donaghue hastened through the gate, excited by Clara's exclamation.

"He keeps a spare key in one of the flower pots," he told her, and they both set to work lifting up or digging in the many plant pots that dotted the front garden.

It was Clara who found the key, underneath a bowl of dead carnations. She grabbed it up and slipped it into the lock. It was rather stiff to turn, but as soon as it did she pushed open the door and ran inside. The front room was just to the right of the hall, and she darted into it, with O'Donaghue just behind. He let out a gasp as he saw what Clara had spotted through the window.

Mr. Johnson was hanging by a piece of washing line from the light fixture in the centre of the room. The weight of the salesman had pulled the fixture partly away from the ceiling, and there was a long crack in the plaster above their heads. Clara reached up for Johnson's hand and felt for a pulse in the wrist. Mr. Johnson was very dead.

"Well, I didn't expect to see that," O'Donaghue took a step back, feeling sick.

Next to Mr. Johnson was a wooden chair. On its seat was a slip of paper. Clara picked it up and read;

I am not an evil man, but I can't bear my shame any longer. I am sorry.

L. Johnson

Clara sighed and replaced the suicide note. She looked up at the bulging face of Mr Johnson and found herself feeling deeply saddened rather than shocked. The poison pen had finally claimed a victim; she had absolutely no doubt that it was the foul contents of the poison pen's letter to Johnson, which had caused the man to hang himself.

"Would you fetch a policeman, Mr O'Donaghue?"

O'Donaghue agreed without hesitation. He was looking extremely pale. When he had disappeared out the door, Clara went around the room having a look for any clues. She had already read the poison pen letter Mr Johnson had received; it was one of the one's handed over to her at Mrs Hampton's gathering. In it, the writer had alleged that Mr Johnson was married and that his wife had left him for another man. Since everyone in the road was convinced Mr Johnson was single, Clara had wondered if the poison pen had made a mistake this time. Now, with Johnson's death, it was clear they had not.

Clara opened a bureau next to the fireplace and went through the drawers. There were a number of invoices, both blank and used, a tally sheet of sales made, and a list of addresses Mr Johnson was due to visit. He roamed across most of the county in pursuit of sales, and a number of train ticket stubs sat in another drawer, clearly waiting to be written down in his expense account. Mr Johnson worked for a company that made agricultural implements, anything from ploughs to hand scythes. He would tour the farms and larger country estates touting his wares, showing off the latest in mechanical hoes or selling a farmer a new shovel. There was a thick, illustrated catalogue on the desk which listed every single item his employers supplied. Clara flicked through it absently and then went back to the bureau. In another drawer she found pencils and postage stamps. In a sliding compartment there was a notepad and, just beneath it, a slip of thick card. Clara pulled out the card and turned it over. It was a photograph of a woman. In black ink, at the very base of the card where a wide white margin created space for text, was the name 'Veronica' and the date 1916.

Clara stared at the woman for a while. The picture was fuzzy and the woman smiled awkwardly at the camera, she looked uncomfortable and stiff. Clara wouldn't be surprised if this was the former Mrs Johnson. In which case, where was she now?

Clara had just replaced the picture and closed the bureau, when a policeman arrived. He took one look at Johnson and swore.

"Excuse me, constable," Clara said to him sternly.

The policeman noticed her for the first time and grabbed off his helmet hurriedly.

"Begging your pardon, miss. I think I ought to send for the Inspector and a doctor. Are you all right, would you like to sit down and have a cup of tea?"

Clara waved him off, she was perfectly all right. She had been shocked to see a pair of feet dangling in mid-air through the window, but by the time she had found the key and entered the house, she had prepared herself for the inevitable. The only thing she really felt was regret. If only she could have talked to Mr Johnson before… well, perhaps he had planned it this way. By hanging himself just before their meeting, he had almost completely ensured his body would be discovered.

Inspector Park-Coombs took an hour to arrive. He had been in Hove due to a burglary in a house belonging to a local Justice of the Peace. He had been asked to personally oversee the investigation, and this meant he was not in a good mood. He never was when local bigwigs threw their weight around near him. Too much of his morning had been spent being berated for the condition of the county and its rising crime rate. Apparently it was all due to the police being lax in their work; the fact that unemployment was crippling the country and poverty was a mounting concern for the vast majority of the working classes, did not come into it, according to the burgled JP. There were days Park-Coombs hated his job.

He stood in the doorway of Mr Johnson's front room and stared at the hanging body. Johnson's face had taken on a rather unpleasant shade of grey. Dr Deáth, Brighton's coroner, was just clipping closed his medical bag as Park-Coombs appeared.

"He is past all help," Deáth said unnecessarily. "I think it is safe to say he died of asphyxia. I shall obviously conduct a post-mortem, considering the circumstances."

"Circumstances?"

Deáth nodded his head to the armchair in the corner of the room and, for the first time, Park-Coombs noticed Clara.

"Ah," was all he said.

Clara had had plenty of time, while waiting for the Inspector, to contemplate Johnson's death. She had been alone for most of that time, the police constable having fled to contact Park-Coombs and O'Donaghue having vanished. With the house to herself she had tried to learn more about the unfortunate Mr Johnson. But, aside from the picture in the bureau, the house held only clues to a bachelor existence. A suitcase stood upstairs, packed ready for his next business-related journey. The bedroom wardrobe held suits and shirts, a spare pair of dress shoes and a selection of smart ties. The bathroom revealed a single toothbrush and pot of tooth powder. There was a shaving kit neatly laid out on a shelf and clean towels hanging from a rail on the wall. In the medicine cabinet there was nothing more exciting than an array of headache and indigestion tablets, all over-the-counter items, nothing prescribed.

Downstairs, in the kitchen, Clara found enough ingredients to prepare simple meals for a couple of days. A loaf in the bread bin looked pretty fresh and Clara began to wonder just how abrupt Johnson's decision to kill himself had been. The larder was stocked with tins of vegetables and Maconochie's stew, and a half bottle of milk stood on a dark shelf corner. Clara found no trace of alcohol anywhere in the house or anything suspicious. Had she come into the house 'cold', she would have described it as the abode of a capable bachelor. Except…

somehow it was too neat, too well-ordered. There was something staged about the whole place, as if someone was putting on a good front but didn't really like or want to live there. The house was not a home. There was none of the debris that marks a place as been well-used and enjoyed. Rather it was like a hotel room, a stopping point in a journey, but not the place where the heart lay.

By the time Clara had returned to the front room, and the body of Johnson, she felt she had come to understand the man a little better. He was a soul that existed, but didn't live. He marked time going from sale to sale, but there was nowhere he actually called home. Clara felt very sad for the man hanging from the light fixture, but that sadness was followed by anger – anger that some cruel soul had chosen to torment a man already in misery by writing him a filthy letter.

"Inspector," Clara had waited until Park-Coombs spotted her before speaking. "As you may imagine, this was not the sort of interview I was expecting to have with Mr Johnson this afternoon."

The Inspector negotiated himself around the dangling body so he could face Clara.

"You had an appointment?"

"At 2pm to be precise, though I was five minutes late."

"I don't think it was your tardiness that caused Mr Johnson to hang himself."

"Nor do I, but I have a good hunch at what did."

Park-Coombs looked at Clara curiously.

"Was he a client of yours?"

"Yes, and I was sworn to the deepest secrecy. But now he is dead and, well, I think that secrecy is forfeit."

"Let's go into the kitchen and you can explain," Park-Coombs glanced over his shoulder. "I prefer to talk somewhere without a dead man peering over my shoulder. You can remove him now Deáth."

The coroner gave a nod. The Inspector and Clara went through into the kitchen and sat down at a small table with three chairs.

"Well, Clara?"

"At the beginning of this week I was contacted by a number of concerned local residents who had received poison pen letters. Mr Johnson was among them."

"Ah."

"Due to the delicate nature of the business, the victims were not inclined to go to the police for fear the scandalous rumours in the letters would be made public. They asked me to discreetly investigate the matter and stop whoever was responsible. Subsequently I have been interviewing those who have received letters, and today I was to speak with Mr Johnson. Upon my arrival no one answered the door and this seemed odd. I peered in the window and, as you can imagine, was rather startled to see my client hanging from the ceiling."

"And what secrets did Mr Johnson have that this poison pen had unearthed?"

"Mr Johnson, unbeknown to most of his neighbours, had been married. But his wife had left him for someone else, or at least that is what the letter implied. I think the poor man felt shamed by the situation and the letter tipped him over the edge."

"But he waited until you were coming before killing himself."

"That, I imagine, was to ensure his body was discovered. Or perhaps, at the last moment, he couldn't face speaking about his failed marriage to me. We shall never know now what he was thinking before he made the decision."

"No."

"Inspector, what is the punishment for writing a poison pen letter?"

Park-Coombs scratched at his chin thoughtfully.

"It is a tricky one. Naturally, if the information in the letter was a lie you could have the writer for defamation of character. But if the information is true, or the manner of the letter is just nasty and not actually making direct accusations, it tends to fall under harassment or causing a public nuisance. If the culprit is discovered, often we will just give them a warning."

"And what about now, with a man dead?"

"No judge in the country would rule that a foul letter was the direct cause of Mr. Johnson's suicide. At best the next of kin might be able to take the writer to court on a civil charge of harassment. They would probably receive a fine, if the case could be proved."

Clara mused on this. It did not seem right that a person who was causing such harm should escape punishment.

"I shall take what I can get," she said after a moment. "From what I have seen, this letter writer is a coward who hides behind anonymity. I suspect a visit from the police alone would be so shameful to them it would put a stop to the matter."

"But you need proof, Clara."

"I'll get it," Clara assured the Inspector. "Don't worry about that."

"And what about other matters?" The Inspector dropped his voice to a whisper and looked to Clara anxiously.

"I am working on that too," Clara promised.

Behind them, in the front room, there was a soft thud as Mr Johnson's body was removed from the light fixing.

Chapter Twenty

At seven o'clock that evening, Clara returned to the hospital. It was now the official visiting hour and there was no receptionist to bark at her as she slipped into the foyer with a number of other visitors and headed upstairs. On the second floor she made her way to Brompton's private room and knocked on the door. There was a muffled response; it could have been an invitation to enter, or it might have been a cough. Clara decided to bank on it being the former and pushed open the door.

Constable Brompton was lying in bed, the top of his head wrapped round with white bandages. He opened his eyes wearily as she entered, the lids fluttering as if the light stung, then he gave a little groan.

"Miss Fitzgerald."

"I am impressed you remember me," there was a chair beside the bed and Clara sat in it. "How are you feeling?"

"Sore. What are you doing here?"

"Making sure you are in one piece," Clara said calmly. "I promised Alfie Ling."

She waited to judge his response. There was no sign of surprise or consternation at the mention of the name, Brompton just closed his eyes to the artificial light in the room.

"Alfie is a good friend."

Clara relaxed. The confirmation assuaged the last of her doubts.

"Mr Brompton, might I say you seem a lot more alert than at our last meeting. I rather feel you took me for a fool last time."

Brompton grimaced a little, and it was no longer because of the bright light.

"I didn't know if I could trust you."

"I gathered that. I might also suggest that you suffered very little in the way of brain damage from your previous accident. You have been masquerading as a simpleton to deter your would-be assassins, am I correct?"

Brompton risked opening his eyes to look at her.

"How much has Ling said?"

"Not a lot, but it was when he said you had worked on 'hush-hush' operations during the war that it dawned on me. A clever man, such as yourself, would recognise when his life was in danger and do what he could to protect himself. At least until he could deal his own blow against his attackers."

"You are quite right," Brompton sighed. "I knew the only chance I had to stay alive was to pretend the accident had robbed me of my wits. I had to make it seem as though I was no longer a threat to my attackers. In any case, you are wrong to say it caused me no brain damage. I suffer the most appalling headaches and I do have lapses in memory, though not as dramatic as I have feigned. Who else knows all this?"

"No one, though I would suspect your attackers will be less comfortable leaving you alive after your visit to the archives. That was extremely risky."

"Yes, but after your visit I was concerned my assailants were checking up on me and I couldn't wait any longer to find answers. I stumbled upon something last year, but the irony is that I am not entirely sure what that 'something' was. I clearly scared someone by asking the wrong question, I simply don't know which of the questions I asked was wrong, if you see what I mean."

"I do," Clara replied. "I also know you are in great danger and I would like to help, if you are prepared to trust me."

"That will put you in danger too," Brompton protested.

"Constable, my life was threatened last year due to someone in the police double-dealing. There is a possibility that, should one of my future cases lead me in the wrong direction, my life will be in danger from this person once again. It is, therefore, for my own self-defence that I intend to root out the crook among your colleagues."

"You know that there is a toad among us, then?"

"Yes."

Brompton closed his eyes again. His head hurt and he felt so tired. Every time he became conscious it seemed only a fragile interval before he descended back into oblivion. He tried to flutter open his eyes once more, but they resisted him. Sleep called irresistibly.

"Before I lose you Brompton, what were you looking for in 'C' section?" Clara asked quickly as Brompton's breathing grew deep and his face relaxed into the softness of sleep.

He mumbled something. She leaned forward over his mouth to try and hear.

"Brillian…" the words were almost silent. Clara leaned closer, but Brompton had fallen to the call of sleep and was gone. All she had was a muttered sentence that sounded like 'brilliant chance'. What did that mean? That if Clara returned to 'C' section she had a good chance of finding an answer? Perhaps there was some clue in the section itself that would aid her. Clara sighed. Or perhaps it had been the ramblings of a semi-conscious man.

Clara sat back down in her seat and checked her watch. There was a good forty minutes left of visiting time and she was reluctant to leave, not so much because she thought Brompton would rouse again, but because she was curious to see if anyone else appeared. Would Brompton's killer put in an appearance, for instance?

Unfortunately she was to be disappointed. No one else showed up during visiting time, not even Brompton's parents. When the bell rang to say it was time for visitors to leave, Clara headed for home feeling she had gained very little that evening, other than discovering that Brompton was not as out-of-his-mind as she first thought.

~~~ * ~~~

Tommy was alone in the parlour when someone rapped at the door. He rolled himself into the hall and opened it before Annie could appear. On the doorstep was Agatha.

"I must talk with you!" she said as soon as she saw him. "I think something awful has happened to the woman in the hotel room next to mine, but when I speak to anyone they think I am a nosy old bat!"

Agatha threw her hands up in the air.

"Oh, well, maybe I am a nosy old bat, but I swear I heard the woman groaning and she did not come down for dinner. We had made an arrangement to dine together, you see, and I am deeply concerned. Did I tell you I worked in a hospital pharmacy? I know the signs of drug abuse and this dear lady is an addict of some description, I am sure. I suspect ether, rather an old-fashioned drug in this day and age, but she is a woman who would have been young when it was fashionable. If she has been taken ill it could be very serious."

Tommy tried to calm her.

"Explain it all to me, from the start," out of the corner of his eye he spotted Annie hiding in the shadows below the staircase.

"The woman, Mrs Welk, arrived at the hotel the same day I did. That first night the dining room was rather crowded and the management politely asked if I would mind allowing Mrs Welk to dine at my table. I said she was most welcome. It was rather dull sitting there on my own. Mrs Welk sat down and we started to talk. I noticed at once the woman was under the influence of something. Her eyes were dull and they darted about the room. She would begin to speak and forget what she was saying. Sometimes she would giggle for no reason. Despite that, she was pleasant company, and we discovered a shared love for card games and small dogs. After that we arranged to dine together most nights," Agatha paused to catch her breath. "At supper today Mrs Welk looked out of sorts. I asked if she had a headache coming on, and she responded that she rather thought she did. After supper she went to her room and I promised to call on her for dinner just before seven. She said she thought she would feel better by then and would be glad of some dinner, having hardly touched her supper. I went to my own room and began typing up some notes. Mrs Welk's room, as it happens, is next to mine and I cannot comment politely on the quality of our shared wall. It is thin, to say the least, and you can hear the person moving about next door. All was silent for a time, I assumed Mrs Welk was resting, then I heard something like a crash, as if a glass had been knocked off a table. I pricked my ears up and a moment later I could have sworn I heard a groan.

"Naturally, I was by now concerned, and I went to Mrs Welk's door, but there was no answer to my knock. I returned to my room and thought things over for a while, it was nearly half past six and I should soon be calling on Mrs Welk for dinner. I really hoped I had allowed my imagination to run away with me and had mistaken a very simple accident for something more dramatic. I went to her door again and knocked. There was still no reply. I called her name, but still nothing. I was very concerned. My instinct was that the dear woman had overdosed herself on something, as I said before she was a person who I felt had a carefree way around drugs. I thought, perhaps, she had taken a sleeping draught or, Heaven forbid, a dose of morphine. It is scandalous what a woman with money can get her hands on. But the hotel manager will not listen to my concerns, Tommy. Mrs Welk could be dying, or already dead, and he simply suggests she did not want to come down for dinner. Can you imagine?"

Tommy could, all too easily.

"I need your help," Agatha concluded. "I thought you might have some influence you could bring to bear."

It was at this moment that an exhausted Clara arrived home. She looked wearily at Agatha and wondered if they were entertaining her again that night. She hoped not. All she really wanted was a hot bath and a quiet dinner.

"The person with influence around here is Clara," Tommy said as soon as he spied his sister. "Maybe she can help? Agatha believes a guest at the hotel she is staying at is seriously ill, but the manager won't listen."

"Ah," Clara said, only half-listening.

"You must come at once Miss Fitzgerald," Agatha seized her arm. "Time is of the essence!"

Clara gave a helpless look to Annie who had emerged from the shadows of the staircase and was standing in the hallway. The girl merely shrugged, what was there to be done when an emergency was afoot. With a tired sigh Clara turned to Agatha.

"You better explain this all to me on the way."

Agatha was staying at the Grand Hotel, a model establishment, aside from the paper thin quality of its internal walls. It hosted tea dances and had a full-time band, along with a pianist who played soothing drawing room numbers during tea. It had recently been refurbished in the latest fashion, with shiny white and red tiles in the foyer and faux pillars decorated with blue palm fronds. It was as if someone had visited an Egyptian hotel, liked it, and then tried to create an anglicised version back home, only without the sunshine or the sand. It looked rather 'overdone' on a dark February evening.

Agatha took Clara straight upstairs to Mrs Welk's room and once again rapped on the door. There was silence. Clara reflected this had rather been the pattern of her last few days. Should she ever knock on a door and someone actually respond, she would be quite stunned.

"You see my dilemma?" Agatha asked.

Clara held up a finger and retreated to Agatha's room. There she found an empty glass and help it against the dividing wall. She pressed her ear against it and listened. For a seemingly endless time neither woman dared to hardly breathe, and then Clara moved from the wall.

"It's faint, but I believe someone is groaning in there."

She offered the glass to Agatha and the procedure was repeated, this time with the other woman listening at the wall. When she finally moved she looked pale.

"I believe you are right."

"Let's speak with that manager again."

Downstairs, the Grand Hotel manager was tucked away in his office. Agatha, acting the indignant guest (which was not difficult considering the circumstances), asked to see him at once. The manager, Mr Miller, was summoned and appeared at the front desk.

Mr Miller had served as manager at the Grand for a decade, and he was used to dealing with whatever perceived outrage his guests felt the need to complain about. He was not, however, used to Clara. As soon as he appeared in his black suit and grey bowtie, she descended on him with irrepressible determination.

"Mr Miller, I insist you summon a doctor at once!"

Miller blinked at her.

"Are you ill?" he tried to place Clara as one of his guests.

"No, but my friend upstairs is. Gravely, I fear. She is lying groaning in her room, and I dare say has little time left. I fear if you do not summon a doctor at once, then it must be the coroner."

There is one thing that no hotel manager wants and that is a scandal. At the words 'coroner' Mr Miller paled a little, Clara dug in the knife.

"I feel it my duty to inform you, that my dear friend may have taken a dangerous substance. If that is the case, the police may need to be summoned as well."

"Police?" Miller almost choked on the word.

"Then again, if we summon the doctor and he transfers her to the hospital, the matter will be out of your hands. Policemen are not that irregular a sight at the hospital to cause alarm, and certainly the coroner would not raise a flutter there. Though, should he appear here…"

"I shall summon a doctor at once!" Miller said without hesitation. "Which guest is unwell?"

"Mrs Welk," Agatha chipped in. "But she has locked her room door and we cannot enter."

"I have the master key," Miller assured them. "I shall only take a moment."

While Miller headed for the telephone, Clara ushered the shaken Agatha to a seat in the foyer. Clara's feet hurt, but she feared that if she sat down she would fall asleep from exhaustion. She compromised by resting her arms on the back of Agatha's chair and balancing one foot off the ground by the toe of her shoe, to take the pressure off her heel. Opposite where she was standing a man in a dinner suit was leaning against a stand of magazines, smoking a cigarette. He was unremarkable, except he was of Chinese descent, and there were few such exotic souls wandering around Brighton. Aside from his Asian origins, he could have been a quintessential English gentleman in his top hat and tails, his hair oiled back and cut short; he smoked elegantly, as if it was an art-form.

Clara realised she was staring and dropped her head. Tiredness had stripped her of her inhibitions. She felt sorry for Mrs Welk, but the call of a warm fire and a comfy chair made it a fleeting sympathy. Drugs were becoming an endemic problem within the country, and there was only so much empathy you could have for a person who deliberately took such dangerous substances. There was something self-destructive about drug addicts that Clara couldn't quite fathom.

Miller returned from his office and flapped around the ladies.

"The doctor will be here shortly. Can I get you

anything? A glass of brandy?"

Agatha shooed him away with one hand.

"I had a dog like him, always fawning and pawing at your feet. Quite distracting," she said.

Clara finally gave in to her weariness and sat down in one of the neat, low-backed armchairs the hotel kept in the foyer. She slipped off a shoe and rubbed her heel.

"It has been quite a day," she said, almost to herself. "I don't suppose you would know if Mrs Welk intended to overdose herself?"

"Suicide? Oh dear, I hadn't considered it."

"It is rather on my mind today," Clara grimaced as her mind went back to Mr Johnson and the cracked ceiling of his front room.

"Excuse me, ladies?"

Clara glanced up. The Chinese gentleman had come over to them. He spoke good English, even if his accent was still strong.

"Did you say, ah, Mrs Welk is sick?"

"Yes," Clara met the man's eyes, trying to get a sense of who he was and what he was doing there.

"She is very sick?"

"Yes, do you know her?" Clara asked.

"Only through business," the man gave her a little bow. "Please excuse me."

With that he left the hotel, not even looking back once.

"What a curious man," Agatha said, a frown on her face.

"Suspicious was more my thinking," Clara pursed her lips. What had the strange foreigner wanted with Mrs Welk? What business could he have with an elderly woman at this time of night in a hotel? The more she considered it, the more uncomfortable she felt.

However, just then the doctor appeared. He had rushed to the hotel as fast as he could and was still doing up his tie as Mr Miller rushed over to him and introduced him to Clara and Agatha.

"Where is the patient then?" he asked impatiently.

The doctor was shown upstairs. Miller had his master key at the ready. Outside Mrs Welk's door Agatha knocked on the woodwork. There was still no answer.

"We can hear her groaning through the wall," Agatha explained to the doctor. "And she missed a dinner engagement. I thought she looked unwell at teatime."

Miller opened the door. The doctor led the way inside, looking reassuringly confident. They entered a sitting room that formed one half of the suite. A long sofa stood with its back to them, to the right the door to the bedroom was open. The room was filled with the odour of sickness and a gasping wheeze could be heard coming from the floor. The sofa blocked their view, but, as they moved around it, Mrs Welk came into sight. She was lying face down on the floor, near to a puddle of her own vomit. A smashed glass was by her foot and a wet patch indicated where the water from it had spilled. The doctor crouched by Mrs Welk and felt her pulse. He carefully turned her over and propped her head on a pillow. She looked a nasty shade of grey and her lips were rather blue.

Agatha glanced at Clara. They had both done their time as nurses during the war and they recognised a serious case when they saw it. Mrs Welk appeared to be struggling to breath, and had been for some time. Without asking, Clara knew her heartbeat would be fluttery and faint, and her pulse would be slower than normal. Mrs Welk was on death's door.

Mr Miller was trembling in the doorway, visions in his mind of policemen and ambulances, and the ghastly newspapermen they would attract like flies to an open wound. Only his professionalism prevented him suggesting they extract Mrs Welk from the hotel as fast as possible.

The doctor sat back on his haunches and looked up at Agatha and Clara, his face was serious.

"She has taken something," he said. "I wouldn't like to

say what exactly it was at this time, but it is a drug of some description. Was she a known addict?"

"I suspected as much," Agatha admitted. "But I thought her drug of choice was ether, this seems more dramatic."

"Ether is not so easy to get hold of these days," the doctor said. "She may have decided to try something new. She is not the first I have seen like this. I suggest we call an ambulance. It might be worth pumping her stomach, then again, if she has inhaled something there is little we can do but wait and see."

Mr Miller made a strangled noise, then composed himself and said he would call an ambulance at once. Agatha sat on the sofa near Mrs Welk and shook her head.

"Poor woman. If only I had known earlier."

Clara set out to explore the small suite. In the bedroom it seemed as if Mrs Welk had been sleeping, and then had rapidly climbed out of bed and headed for the sitting room, perhaps when she began to struggle to breathe. The bed clothes were in a tangled mess on the floor and a lamp had been knocked on its side as she had panicked and clambered out of bed. Clara opened the bedside table drawer, looking for suspicious contents. There was nothing but a Bible provided by the hotel.

Next to the bedroom was a private bathroom, and this proved more illuminating. There was a night bag on a shelf containing a range of pill bottles, everything from a daily laxative to harmless vitamin pills. There were also several pill boxes sitting on the edge of the sink. Clara opened each one, looking for a substance she could not place. While most seemed to contain aspirin or digestion aids, one opened to reveal a strange white powder. Clara carried the pill box through to the doctor and showed it to him. He glanced at the contents, dipped his finger in them and then placed a miniscule amount on his tongue. He savoured it for a moment.

"Cocaine," he said. "Yes, a large dose of that could

leave a person in a mess like this."

Agatha looked close to tears. Clara clicked closed the lid of the box. Her mind was on the Chinese man in the foyer and his mention of business with Mrs Welk. It had to be said that a lot of the drug trade, be it opium, heroin or cocaine, had an oriental source. She wondered if she had just met an upmarket drug dealer.

Mr Miller appeared back at the doorway.

"I have called for an ambulance, it shall meet us at the kitchen entrance."

Agatha glowered at him, and the man shrunk a little from the force of the look. Clara placed a restraining hand on her shoulder. It might be just as well for all concerned if Mrs Welk was discreetly taken to hospital. The poor woman would not want her secret exposed to the world.

The ambulance arrived within fifteen minutes and Mrs Welk was taken away on a stretcher. She looked extremely pale and was breathing shallowly. The doctor appeared to be pessimistic about her chances of survival. Clara escorted Agatha to her room and ordered her a brandy from room service.

"Did you ever see a soldier addicted to cocaine during the war?" Agatha asked her.

"No," Clara admitted. "I have heard about it. I saw plenty of men addicted to morphine."

"Just as bad," Agatha nodded. "I met one or two who had developed a cocaine habit. It wasn't pretty."

"That man who spoke to us about Mrs Welk, had you ever seen him before?"

"The Oriental?" Agatha shook her head. "I would have remembered."

Clara advised Agatha to get some rest and then headed for home. She was exhausted and hungry, and deeply concerned. She was under no illusions that Brighton had avoided succumbing to the drug scandal that was affecting much of the country; they were too close to London for that. The national papers regularly discussed the problem which, according to them, was becoming an epidemic. But to see it so close to hand – in a respectable hotel – made her shudder. It was like some monster had crawled up from the pit where it belonged and into the sunlight. The whole business had left a very nasty taste in her mouth.

Chapter Twenty-One

Clara made a leisurely start to Saturday morning. There had been snow in the night and she was not inclined to go out until the usual traffic had cleared at least some of the roads. Besides, she was still tired from the night before. She drank two cups of tea and ate the eggs and bacon Annie had insisted on cooking for her. Annie was complaining that Clara looked peaky and had lost some weight. Clara felt that, according to the fashion standards of the day, she could easily afford the weight loss, but Annie was appalled. She came from a traditional family of hard-working women who knew that an ample body was the best insurance against the deadliest of winter diseases. Annie had no time for magazines that instructed woman to reduce themselves to skeletons. She was convinced one good bout of fever would kill off half the fashionable female gender. As she had no intention of Clara being part of that number (and having been deeply worried about her during her illness), she was determined to feed her up. For that matter, Tommy was coming under her eagle gaze too, though, in his case, he actually liked being stuffed with food. To Annie's alarm (and Clara's envy), Tommy failed to put on a single pound despite the copious amounts of food Annie fed him.

Clara wrapped herself up well in a warm coat and scarf at ten o'clock and set out on her first mission of the morning, which she was not particularly looking forward to. Most of the roads had been cleared by the early morning carts, but the pavements were still deep in snow and Clara took her time, picking her steps carefully. Her mind briefly turned to Mrs Welk; had she survived the night?

She walked past Mr Johnson's house and another pang of sadness filled her, that was swiftly followed by anger and, by the time she reached the front door of the Cotterley sisters' home, she was feeling quite furious. The harm and evil these three women had caused, all out of spite, was unspeakable, and she knew full well that little would be done about them. But, if she could stop the letters, that would be something. She rapped hard on the door.

No one answered. She cast her eyes to the bay window on her right and a face vanished behind a curtain. She knocked again, harder. There was still silence inside. The Cotterleys were not going to answer the door. Clara felt even angrier at the sight of such cowardly behaviour. How was she supposed to confront the Cotterleys if they would not even come to the door? She was about to leave and rethink her plan when she heard footsteps crunching behind her.

She turned to see a very thin woman with a time-worn face standing just inside the garden gate. She was dressed all in grey and had a large basket gripped by the handle in both hands. Weary, puffy eyes looked at Clara.

"They won't answer."

"I need to speak with them," Clara insisted. "Are you Mrs Grimes?"

"Yes," Mrs Grimes gave a start. "How did you know?"

"I was told you brought the Cotterleys their shopping. If I cannot speak with them, could I speak with you for a moment? It is very important."

Mrs Grimes chewed on her lip, looking anxiously at

the door.

"What have they done?" she asked, after a long moment.

"Aside from writing some appalling letters, they are very much morally responsible for the untimely death of Mr Johnson."

"Poor man," Mrs Grimes sighed, staring down into her basket. "Why don't we go back to my house? It is just a couple of roads away."

Mrs Grimes led Clara to a respectable terrace, considerably bigger than the one occupied by the Cotterleys. She took Clara in through the back door and into a warm kitchen. A beef pudding was slowly boiling in a pan and there was a smell of freshly baked cake. Mrs Grimes clattered tea cups down from a shelf before offering to take Clara's coat.

"Did you know about the poison pen letters?" Clara asked when they were settled.

"I had heard rumours, but everyone is being very discreet about it. It hadn't occurred to me that my mother or aunts could be involved."

"Your mother's handwriting gave them away. It was recognised," though not by Miss Wicks, Clara conceded to herself, which was worrying. "There were other clues too."

"Oh dear," Mrs Grimes groaned a little. "Thomas will be furious. He hates them already. He will try and insist I never see them again. But, I can't abandon them, can I? Who would do their shopping?"

Clara felt inclined to say that, perhaps, if the Cotterley sisters had to do their own shopping and leave the house, they would have less time for venting their spite on the innocent. Then again, maybe not.

"Is shopping the only thing you do for them?"

"No," Mrs Grimes pulled a face. "I post letters for them too. I suppose I posted those letters."

Mrs Grimes gave a groan.

"Are the Cotterley sisters ill, Mrs Grimes?"

"Only the complaints of old age. A little arthritis here and there. Oh, but you mean, why don't they leave the house?" Mrs Grimes gave this some thought. "I suppose it is because they are afraid of people. They don't want to talk to anyone, in case someone asks them a difficult question. They have always had extremely high expectations and are very proud. But pride can so easily turn to shame, don't you think? They are ashamed of so many things in their lives, not least my own daughter's indiscretion, which they encouraged. That shame keeps them housebound. They don't want to let the outside world in, for fear it would remind them of their failings."

"Well, they have invited me into their lives through these letters."

"Yes, I suppose they didn't think of that."

"I need to speak with them. I hope a quiet chat will stop the letters. If I must I will take this matter to the police," Clara avoided adding that she didn't have enough evidence to get the police involved.

"They would hate that."

"Which is why I hoped to talk to them before it came to that. They have done a dreadful thing, and it has cost one man his life."

"I'm so sorry," Mrs Grimes looked close to tears. "If I had known I never would have posted those letters."

"Please, I am not accusing you," Clara reassured her, but the woman still looked distressed. Clara tried to distract her. "I don't suppose you have a sample of your mother's handwriting I could compare to the letters?"

Mrs Grimes left the table and went to a Welsh dresser standing against one wall. She rummaged in a drawer and produced a handful of letters. She placed them on the table.

"These are a few years old, from when my mother still took holidays. She would write to me every day. But I also have this," she drew a handwritten shopping list from her pocket.

Clara studied the letters and the list for a few

moments. The writing was identical to that she had seen on the poison pen letters.

"Might I take the shopping list and one of the letters?"

Mrs Grimes nodded. She looked worn down, all her strength gone from her. She sat down quietly, staring at a knot in the woodwork of her kitchen table.

"I am sorry to ask, but could you get me inside the Cotterley house to speak with the sisters?"

Mrs Grimes pulled another face. No doubt she was thinking of the reprimands and lectures she would receive for weeks after for helping Clara inside. Clara found it hard to imagine putting up with such people, even if they were close kin. But Mrs Grimes clearly felt obligated to them. After a long silence Mrs Grimes looked up.

"I will help you, only because they have done such an awful thing and they need to be stopped. They destroy lives, not through violence, but through their insidious lies and false promises. I wish I had recognised their nature sooner, maybe Ellen could have been spared their influence," a tear fell down Mrs Grimes' face. "I know her disgrace was in part their doing. Ellen met Major Dennis at a Victory ball. He had more interest in her than she did in him, at least at first. But she told my mother and aunts and they turned her head with ideas that she would be the envy of all the local girls as a Major's wife. They imagined he had a lot of money too. None of them guessed he was married, and when it was discovered, well, my aunts saw that as no real issue. He clearly no longer loved his wife, or why was he courting Ellen?

"I found out too late what was going on. Ellen made a fool of herself and everyone learned of it, Mrs Dennis made sure of that. And then the good Major just abandoned her for some flat-chested blonde with a wealthy daddy. I was heartbroken. Thomas, my husband, has not spoken to Ellen since the day it all came out."

Mrs Grimes choked back a sob.

"They seem to keep bringing hardship upon me," she shook her head. "People say I should have nothing to do with them, but they are family. I know I am a fool."

"Let me speak with them and, hopefully, there will be no need to take this further," Clara was still sorely tempted to hand the Cotterleys over to the police, but she was beginning to see it would do no real good and would probably only bring harm on those already affected by the Cotterleys' maliciousness. Instead, she would see to it that the sisters suffered a punishment far worse to them than a fine handed down by a judge. They would be shamed in front of their neighbours.

Mrs Grimes escorted Clara back to the Cotterley house. She explained on the way that she had her own key and would let them both in. She also warned Clara to expect to be verbally assaulted the second she stepped over the threshold. Clara was prepared for that and, in response, she was armed with her own sense of indignation and righteous fury. Besides, she had dealt with gangsters in the past, how scary could three little old ladies be?

Mrs Grimes took them to the front door, explaining that the backyard was virtually impassable these days. The weeds and shrubs had taken it over, the sisters were not inclined to gardening and the chore used to fall on Mr Grimes' shoulders. But the scandal over Ellen had finished that. Mrs Grimes looked quite ashamed that her husband would so neglect her mother and aunts. Clara, however, could fully understand the man's principles. She was beginning to recognise Mrs Grimes as one of life's martyrs; in fact, it was a trend that seemed to run through the Cotterley family. She was bowed down by her misery and constantly blamed others for her misfortune when, in reality, much of it was of her own making. She could, at any moment, remove herself from the presence of the Cotterleys and most of her neighbours would understand the decision. But she wouldn't do that. Suffering was a badge of honour for her, one she wore with pride.

The key turned in the lock and the door swung open.

The hallway was dark. A staircase ran up the left hand wall. Clara nipped in behind Mrs Grimes and pulled the door closed. Now she was truly trapped inside the lion's den.

"Hello?" Mrs Grimes called out.

"Here!" a shrill voice cried from the back parlour.

Mrs Grimes went to the doorway. Three old women were sat around a brightly burning fire.

"We expected you earlier. Maggie looked out the window when she heard someone knock, thinking you had mislaid your key, but it was that ghastly female detective who has been snooping around," Heather Cotterley declared to her daughter.

As she spoke Mrs Grimes moved to one side and Clara appeared in the doorway. There was a collective gasp from the old women.

"What have you done?" Heather scowled at her daughter.

Mrs Grimes was cowed and hung her head. Clara merely looked at the scene before her and remembered the part in Macbeth where the eponymous main character stumbles over the three witches. The lack of a cauldron was the only missing element.

"Good morning ladies," she said.

"And you can leave at once!" the woman on the right of the fire pointed a crooked finger at Clara. "I have seen you peering in windows! Wicked girl! Wicked!"

"I have no intention of leaving," Clara said firmly. "I have an important matter to discuss with you all."

"You can say nothing we want to hear, get out of our house!" Heather growled. "We shall have no silly, nosy girl interfering in our lives!"

"I am afraid your own actions have brought me here," Clara said quite calmly, she was actually starting to enjoy herself. "I suppose I ought to thank you for my letter."

"Letter?" Heather snorted. "We never sent you a letter."

But she looked shaken; there had been a hesitation

before she spoke.

"I think you did," Clara responded. "As you sent the others. If we want to talk about wickedness, I think we need look no further than yourselves."

"What lies! Get your filthy tongue out of my house!" one of the Cotterleys – the oldest by Clara's guess – was gesticulating at her with a clenched fist and spitting out her words. "You are just a witch young lady, a witch!"

Heather was twitching with bottled fury, her head trembled strangely, like it was about to fall off. Clara knew she had hit a nerve.

"Shall we cease the name calling? It really is quite childish," she said firmly. "Let me lay my cards on the table. I have been given a series of vile letters written to people in this road, accusing them of terrible things. I have also been given a sample of your handwriting, Heather Cotterley, and I have a witness who will testify that she believes the letter written to her daughter could only have been sent by you."

Maggie Cotterley gave a nasty hiss.

"Maud Harris!"

Clara smiled. Another nail in the coffin. The women were really quite foolish in their spite.

"I have all the evidence I need to go to the police and demand they arrest you all for causing a nuisance."

Heather Cotterley sank back into her chair, looking stunned. The only person to speak was the third sister.

"You evil cow!" she spat, "Attacking innocent old ladies who just want to be left alone…"

"Diana, be quiet," Heather snapped.

Diana, the third and eldest Cotterley sister, glowered in response.

"You always lacked backbone," she snapped back at her sister. "She has nothing but suspicions. Let her go to the police, they will do nothing!"

"On the contrary, they will come to this house and press charges against you. You will all have to appear in court, though Heather, as the author of the letters, will be deemed the most culpable."

"Hah, you can threaten us all you want…"

"Diana!" Heather growled. "She has caught us out!"

Diana glared at her sisters, an evil look coming across her face. She folded her crabbed hands over her chest.

"I didn't write any letters. Don't know what she is talking about," she said with a straight face, looking directly into Heather's eyes.

"So that's how it is? Throw me to the lions, would you?" Heather retorted. "Is that what sisterly love comes down to?"

Diana gave a shrug and a complacent look, indicating she was unmoved. Clara found the anger and hatred between the sisters remarkable; they seemed to despise each other as much as they despised their neighbours. How anyone could willingly live in such an unpleasant household astounded her, though it did go some way to explaining why the sisters had turned all their negativity into letter writing. It was clearly a release from the misery of their existence together.

"I will only go to the police if I have to," Clara said, restoring their attention to her. "My sole goal in coming here was to inform you the game was up and that you are to stop this evil nonsense at once."

"How can the truth be evil?" Maggie said abruptly. "Secrets are evil, truth is not."

"It is when you warp it to your own designs," Clara corrected her. "Besides, much of your prose was little better than vicious gossip. The truth of your words was extremely limited."

"People should be more honest then, and that would prevent gossip," Heather was regaining some of her composure.

Clara was determined she would not slip the noose.

"Gossip is the work of bored, sad little people who are so unhappy in their lives they take it out on others."

"Unhappy?" Heather snapped. "You are the one who is unhappy, running around playing detective. I know your sort, young lady, can't find a decent man so you poke your nose into everyone else's affairs."

"I do not care what you think," Clara said, realising at the same instant that she meant the words too. "I have no need for your approval or, for that matter, anyone else's. I help people, which is more than can be said for you."

"Oh, so you are better than us?" Heather laughed. "That is rich. I imagine you think you are being very clever. Well, let me tell you, any woman with a brain would see you and feel embarrassed to share the same gender! I have never known such a disgrace to walk into my house before!"

"I'm sorry you feel that way. Perhaps if you had realised there was more to being a woman than simply finding a husband and having children, you would not be so bitter now. But that is really not my problem. My problem is that you have spent your time persecuting your neighbours. You have driven one man to his death. Mr Johnson hung himself because of the letter you sent."

Diana gave a malicious smile.

"Did he, now? Man had no courage, good riddance."

The look Clara turned on the nasty old woman actually gave Diana cause to shrink back a little.

"What business was it of yours? Enough of this! You are clearly irredeemable, the lot of you. I shall leave this house and inform all your neighbours of what you have been doing and, should you send any more letters, they will know at once where to come to respond to them."

"You can't do that," Maggie pressed her hands to her mouth. "They will all know. They will talk about us."

"As you deserve," Clara scowled. "You are guilty of murder in my eyes, but a court of law will never convict you of it. All I can do is make your guilt known to your neighbours, and hope the shame of being so discovered will temper your actions in the future."

"You can't do that, please," Maggie begged. "They will come to the door!"

"And what did you expect when you began this

malicious spree of letter writing? You invade their homes and their lives. They have the right to respond."

The sisters fell into silence. There was nothing else to say. Not one of them was prepared to say they were sorry for what they had done (not that any one of them was sorry), but still, the thought of being discovered was awful.

"The only question I have is why you changed your handwriting for Miss Wicks? All the other letters were clearly written by Heather. So why was Miss Wicks' letter different?" Clara asked.

Maggie gave her a puzzled look.

"We never wrote one of the letters to Miss Wicks."

"Maggie, you are an idiot," Diana wagged a gnarled finger at her.

"Why?" Maggie's tear-filled eyes turned to her sister.

"You just implied you had written the others," Clara explained, not that such a mild statement would stand up in court, of course.

"But…" Maggie glanced at Heather. "I thought she knew we had written the letters?"

"She suspected, you just confirmed it," Heather told her coldly.

Maggie put her hands back to her mouth and winced.

"Maggie is right on one thing," Heather, the most rational of the three, looked at Clara. "We have never written anything malicious to Miss Wicks."

Clara filed that piece of information away. So who had written Miss Wicks' letter?

Mrs Grimes was by now looking deeply upset and agitated. She was convinced that, sooner or later, her mother and aunts would turn on her for bringing Clara into their house. She desperately wanted to make her exit. Clara had achieved all she could with the Cotterleys, anyway. They were neither remorseful nor inclined to apologise for their actions, but she was confident they would not risk writing anymore letters. The result would be a crowd of angry people on their doorstep, and they wouldn't want that. Clara decided it was time to leave.

Mrs Grimes showed her out. The Cotterleys were silent. Outside the front door Mrs Grimes burst into tears.

"I shall never be welcome here again," she sobbed.

Clara hardly thought that much of a thing to cry over. She patted the woman's arm comfortingly.

"Never mind, they will still need their shopping."

Mrs Grimes took this as a minor consolation. Clara left her mulling over the future and headed directly to Mrs Wilton. There would be no one better to spread the discoveries she had made then the biggest gossip in town. At least Mrs Wilton didn't use her talents maliciously – well, mostly.

She was met at Mrs Wilton's door by a maid of better class and manners than Mrs Wilton's last one, and was shown into a sitting room. Mrs Wilton had a villa on the cliffs overlooking the sea, and the rooms were considerably brighter and airier than those Clara had just left. She stood at the window and stared out at the grey sea, awaiting Mrs Wilton. The woman arrived wearing a pinny and gardening gloves.

"I was making a start on the flowers for this month's arrangements in church," she explained. "It is challenging to get a suitably attractive display with so little growing at the moment."

Clara acknowledged that would be a problem for Brighton's avid flower arrangers.

"I have news."

"I thought you might. After that business with Mr Johnson, I hoped you would be able to resolve matters swiftly. I quite liked the poor man. He sold me a lovely green house last year."

"Well, I know who has been writing the letters and I have just approached them and insisted they stop. You are free to tell everyone that the Cotterley sisters were behind this whole fiasco."

"Those heartless beasts!" Mrs Wilton's mouth

dropped. "I knew they had long ago lost their souls, but to think they were behind such evil! What did they say?"

"Very little. They denied it, but the evidence was overwhelming. Should the letters reappear you will know who to complain to. I have told them I will be informing all their neighbours of their actions."

"I bet that displeased them!"

"They were not impressed," Clara smiled. "One odd thing, however. They deny sending a letter to Miss Wicks, yet she clearly received one."

"She came to the meeting," Mrs Wilton nodded. "Now you mention it, it does strike me as strange she would receive a nasty letter from them. The Cotterleys were always staunch allies with Miss Wicks. Peas in a pod, you might argue. I believe Miss Wicks took against them when they shut themselves away and stopped writing to her. They failed to send her a Christmas card one year and she took it rather badly. But, of course, nothing she could do with them shut away in their house. I don't think harsh words were ever spoken. Miss Wicks just accepted they had abandoned her."

"That would explain her response when I mentioned their names to her. But if they are not responsible for Miss Wicks' letter, then the only other possibility is that someone else used the excuse of the poison pen letters to write their own unpleasant missive to her."

"Oh no, does that mean we have another letter writer to worry about?"

"I doubt it. I think this was a one off act of spitefulness or even revenge. Has Miss Wicks caused anyone great offence?"

"She is hardly the most pleasant of women," Mrs Wilton grimaced. "That being said, she rarely causes real trouble. I could think of a list of people she has had cause to complain to, but no one I could specifically say held a grudge against her."

"Then I shall have to pay her another call," Clara decided reluctantly. "Well, I must get on Mrs Wilton.

Can I rely on you to spread the word?"

"Naturally," Mrs Wilton assured her. "Thank you, my dear."

Clara took her leave and headed into town. Miss Wicks could wait; she had other, much more serious, business to attend to.

Chapter Twenty-Two

The police station was relatively quiet for a Saturday. Clara showed her special identification card that allowed her access to the archives, and the Desk Sergeant reluctantly allowed her through. Clara mused that, should the Desk Sergeant prove to be the traitor in the ranks, it would be her pleasure to unmask him. She doubted she was that lucky.

She headed down to the archives and found herself standing on the spot where she had found Constable Brompton. The concrete floor had been scrubbed and there was no trace of blood, but there was still a clear space that indicated where he had been sitting. Poor Brompton, what had he discovered? Clara stepped around the spot and was about to head to 'C' section, when she was surprised to see she was not alone. A young man was taking files out of boxes. He was in police uniform, but had discarded his jacket while working in the basement. The archives room being right next to the boiler room meant it was the warmest place in the station. In fact, it was rather overheated, so it was natural to discard the jacket.

"Good morning," Clara said.

The young man looked up. He had brown hair and

hazel eyes. His smile was pleasant.

"Good morning, you must be Miss Fitzgerald."

Clara admitted she was.

"I'm Constable Tilney. They sent me down to sort some files. It's quiet today."

"I noticed."

Tilney picked up a stack of cardboard folders he had just finished sorting from the box.

"Excuse me, would you, these belong at the far end," Trimley headed towards the back of the room, while Clara headed in the opposite direction.

'C' section was one long row of shelves lined with boxes from floor to ceiling. Clara looked at the amount of files sitting on the shelves and her heart sank. Lost needles and haystacks sprang to mind. There were also lots of unsorted boxes of files on the floor before the shelves. As Clara tried to edge nearer to the shelved files her foot caught on one of these loose boxes and caused it to tip over. Files scattered across the floor. Clara sighed and bent down to right the box. It was as she did so, that she noticed the small red dot on the very edge of the box. She peered a little closer. It was a speck of blood. This was the box Brompton had been leaning over when he was struck on the head! Which meant one of these scattered files might be just the one he was looking for!

Clara started to gather up the files, reading the names on them as she went. None rang any particular bell until she picked one up with the name 'Chang' written on it. The first name, written just after the surname in smaller letters, was 'Brilliant'.

Clara stared at the file. Brompton had not been telling her she had a good chance of finding the clue to his assault in the files, he had been giving her the name of the person she should be looking for. Brilliant Chang.

Opening the file there was a headshot of an Asian man, turned slightly away from the camera and clearly taken at some social event, for he was in evening dress. It was the man Clara had met in the foyer of the hotel asking after

Mrs Welk. Rapidly she read the details in the file. Male. Asian. Aged 35. 5ft 6in. Resided in England since 1907. Arrested for supplying cocaine 1908, 1909, 1910. Last conviction 1910, two years hard labour. Suspected of running drug trafficking ring.

The file was flimsy and low on information after 1910, except for a list of sightings of Chang at various high class parties and society meetings. He was also implicated in the untimely death of the actress Billie Carleton (who had perished from a drug overdose), but once again Chang had managed to slip the grasp of the authorities. Now he had turned up in Brighton and his name was on Constable Brompton's lips. A coincidence? Clara didn't think so.

Clara carefully gathered up the other folders and put them back in the box, as she did so she heard footsteps approaching. She slipped Brilliant Chang's file under her coat just as Tilney came around the corner. He saw her righting the box she had knocked over.

"Sorry, constable," Clara beamed at him. "I caught the box with my foot. I've put them back as they were."

"It's a bit cluttered in here," Tilney nodded. "Were you looking for something in particular?"

"Why, yes," Clara had already thought up the perfect excuse. "I was hoping to find a police report on an accident that happened back in the 1870s. A barge sank and people drowned. One of the men on board had the name of Cotterley."

"1870s?" Constable Tilney pursed his lips. "That's a long while back. Sometimes our older records are destroyed or sent to our central archives in London."

Tilney moved between the boxes and thumbed along the shelf. Clara stood pretending to be patiently waiting when, in fact, she was burning with nerves that he might notice she had slipped a file beneath her coat. In the hot room it was rather odd she should still be wearing it and she was beginning to overheat.

"Ah, Cotterley," Tilney took down a file and presented

it to Clara. "This looks like it."

Clara accepted the folder and flicked it open with the pretence of interest. Had she wanted to further delve into the Cotterleys' tragic past she would have been sorely disappointed. The file contained a single sheet of paper with a very brief report on the barge accident. There was a reference number for further information. Clara couldn't help herself.

"What does this mean, Constable Tilney?"

Tilney glanced at the number.

"That means a full accident report was filed separately, but not here, I'm afraid. You'll have to ask the Inspector if you can have access to our secondary archive at the coroner's office. We are rather overwhelmed by paperwork," he indicated the room. "So we had to create a second archive."

Clara needed to hear no more. She had just been given a first class excuse to pop up to see the Inspector.

"Thank you for your help, constable. I shall go see the Inspector at once. This Cotterley business could be quite important," she handed him back the folder. "Good morning."

With some relief she exited the archives and escaped up to the ground floor. The Desk Sergeant gave her his usual unpleasant scowl.

"Is the Inspector in his office?" Clara asked.

"Not on a Saturday, unless he has to be." the Desk Sergeant grumbled, clearly implying that it was all right for some.

Fortunately, Clara knew the Inspector's home address. Normally she would not descend on him uninvited on a weekend, but she had a feeling he would want to know about her discovery. She gave the Desk Sergeant her brightest smile and headed outside.

By the time she reached the Inspector's terrace house it was lunchtime, and she almost hesitated to knock, in case he was eating. But the urgency of the file she had, theoretically, stolen, forced her hand. She rapped on the door and hoped that Mrs Park-Coombs was forgiving. It was, in fact, the Inspector who opened the door.

"Clara?"

"I hope I am not interrupting, but I think I have a lead," Clara was breathless with the seriousness of the matter.

The Inspector only gaped at her for a second, then invited her in. He had just been starting on a cold lunch of boiled eggs and dripping on bread, left behind by his wife who had gone to see her sister. He offered a share to Clara, but she was too anxious to eat. As they settled at the small folding table where the Inspector had set his lunch, she took the Chang folder from under her coat and placed it on the table.

"I know I stole it, but I felt it was urgent. This is the file Brompton was looking for when he was attacked."

"How can you be sure?" the Inspector turned the folder to face him.

"He told me, or rather he mumbled it. I might have been more uncertain about it myself, if it was not for the fact that I saw Brilliant Chang in person just the other night."

The Inspector glanced up from the file sharply.

"Where?"

"The Grand Hotel. I shall explain quickly. A lady at the hotel was taken ill, I happen to have a friend also staying at the hotel who was convinced this said lady was a drug addict. We were awaiting the arrival of a doctor when I spotted this man in the foyer. More importantly, when he heard me mention the name of the lady taken ill, he enquired after her, saying he had business with her. When he heard we were summoning a doctor he vanished."

"Brilliant Chang," Park-Coombs sighed. "I know the name. Drug dealing has become a big and very lucrative business. If anyone was going to have the funds to pay off one of my constables it would be this Chang fellow."

"So you believe me?"

"I do. But this brings us no closer to finding the cuckoo in our nest."

"What of the men on that list you gave me?" Clara drew the list from her notebook. "These three men were all present when Razor Brown escaped. Perhaps we can see some connection between them and Chang?"

"Perhaps," Park-Coombs said dubiously. He was feeling rather defeated by the whole matter. One of his men had betrayed the police and he was taking it very personally.

"Constable Edgar Bunn," Clara read aloud.

"Bunn is a relatively new recruit. Rather green, but harmless enough, as far as I can see. He was off-duty the day Brompton was attacked at the station."

"Then he is probably not our man. The person who attacked Brompton had to have been at the station on the day he snuck into the archives."

"Unless the attacker has an accomplice."

"Let's not make life too complicated just yet, Inspector. What of Constable Robert Jones?"

"Welshman. Came to Brighton just after the war. He wants to be a detective. Very keen lad. He was very concerned when Billy Brown escaped, I remember that well," the Inspector nodded. "It was Jones who reported the matter to me. He noticed Brown was missing when he went to check on the cells."

"He seems unlikely as the person responsible, then?"

The Inspector shrugged.

"A double bluff is always possible."

"Well, the last name is, oh," Clara smiled in recognition. "Constable John Tilney. I just met him in your archives while I was, ahem, stealing this file on Chang."

Inspector Park-Coombs' head shot up.

"You met Tilney?"

"Yes. He said he was sorting files."

"But, today is his day off," the Inspector said in surprise.

"Are you sure?"

"I approved the work roster for this week myself. The men don't get much time off, we are rather short-handed. But I try to ensure they have a least one whole day a month," the Inspector had a thoughtful look on his face. "Tilney is not the sort to come in on his day off, and certainly not to sort files."

"Unless you have another constable named Tilney, this was the man who introduced himself to me in the archives," Clara said. "Tell me more about him."

"John Tilney joined the police in 1916, when we were rather desperate for men. I dare say he aimed to avoid the army, but perhaps that is too harsh. He is an adequate constable. Does his duty. I can't say he stands out, but there are quite a few constables like that. I always felt he was marking time," Park-Coombs mused. "Likes the good things in life, does Tilney. Always buying new hats and bowties. And chocolate, he is very fond of good chocolate. Not to mention the ladies. I am amazed he is not dallying with one of his female friends today. That is how Tilney usually spends his free time."

"Then he is a man who likes money?" Clara queried. "A man who might find a constable's wages a little restrictive? How did he get on with Brompton?"

Park-Coombs shook his head.

"I don't think they associated much. They were too different. Brompton was a policeman to the core. Tilney does what he has to, and no more."

"Yet, there he is on his day off. Helping with the filing," Clara hardly needed to make her tone sound suggestive to imply what she was thinking.

"It is curious."

"More than curious. I would say suspicious."

The Inspector tapped his fingers on the table.

"Tilney regularly patrols along the seafront. Where was that hotel you said you saw Chang?"

"The Grand."

"Tilney goes past that on a nightly basis," the fingers

tap-tapped. "It was one of the cases Tilney had worked on, where I first noted a discrepancy. A witness statement had gone missing. I knew because I had happened to look at the file previously."

"Tilney and Chang," Clara considered. "He seems our best suspect."

"But even if he is the culprit, we have no real evidence against him."

"No," Clara admitted. "We don't. But that doesn't mean we can't catch him."

"What is on your mind?" the Inspector asked.

"If we can't arrest Tilney, then we must lure him out. We need him to give us the evidence of his association with Chang," Clara smiled. "We must set a trap. Brompton will be our bait."

"And how will this trap work?"

"Word will circulate at the police station that Brompton has awoken and remembers who attacked him. It shall be emphasised that you are going to take his statement in person. The assailant, be it Tilney or not, will hopefully panic and attempt to silence Brompton once and for all, before you can visit him. We need merely wait for his arrival."

"All very good, but if I start spreading such rumours at the station someone will smell a rat."

"I wasn't thinking of you, Inspector, as our blabber-mouth. I have someone else in mind."

Park-Coombs looked at her curiously.

"Who?"

Clara winked.

"Brompton's very own avenging angel."

Chapter Twenty-Three

Clara arrived home just after two o'clock, having set her plan into action. She would need to be at the hospital shortly, but was hoping to have time to change her clothes and eat a little lunch before leaving. As she stepped in the front door, however, she was greeted by a fraught Oliver Bankes.

"Clara, we must hurry!" he said urgently. "I'll explain on the way."

He grabbed her arm as Clara began to protest. He had pulled her out the door and onto the pavement before Clara was able to yank her arm away.

"Oliver Bankes!"

"My father has lost his mind," Oliver said quickly. "So have half of his neighbours. After they heard who has been sending the letters, they formed a mob and are headed over, right this instant, to the Cotterley house, to give them a piece of their mind. I tried to talk some sense into my father, but it was no good. I think only you will be able to stop this mess before it gets out of hand."

Clara had not anticipated this. She suddenly felt guilty for allowing Mrs Wilton to spread the word of who was behind the letters. She should have called a meeting herself and spoken in person. That would have given her a chance to dispel any plans for retribution.

"Quickly then!" she told Oliver.

They ran as fast as they could to the Cotterley house; Clara yet again regretting her shoes. Outside the old ladies' home was a gang of people. Clara counted six of them, including Mr Summerton and Oliver's father. Mrs Wilton was standing to one side flapping her hands and asking people to behave in a rational manner. Her words were clearly falling on deaf ears. Clara gave herself a moment to catch her breath and assess the situation. The gaggle of complainants had not achieved much, as yet. They were stood in the front garden of the Cotterley house making a lot of noise and occasionally thrusting someone forward to hammer on the door. But these were not law-breakers or rioters; they were angry people, who still remained polite enough to resist doing any real harm. However, that did not make the situation any less frightening for the Cotterleys.

Clara asked for Oliver to give her a hand and, with a slight wobble, hoisted herself onto the top of the low brick wall that ran outside the Cotterleys' garden.

"Gentlemen! Ladies!" she called out, a couple of heads turned towards her. "May I have your attention?"

No one answered her, everyone was muttering among themselves.

"Or must I call the police and ask them to arrest you for disturbing the peace?"

That quelled them. There were a couple of voices of protest, but mostly everyone was now paying attention to Clara.

"Good," she said. "Now, what precisely are you attempting to achieve here?"

"We are going to give them a piece of our minds!" Mr Summerton declared angrily.

"And you really think they are going to answer a door to an angry mob? Would you?"

"We shall make them!" a woman said.

"How?" Clara asked quite calmly, even if she was

having to keep a very careful eye on her footing on the wall. "Will you break down the door?"

There was a sullen silence.

"This is a pointless exercise. Now, really, is this any way for decent, polite folk to behave?"

"We wanted to have our say, to tell them how upsetting their letters were," Mr Summerton answered.

"That is understandable," Clara replied. "And I am certain your presence here has impressed upon the Cotterleys how angry those letters have made you. But we have to remember we are dealing with three elderly ladies. Spiteful ladies, yes, but still old and vulnerable. They are no doubt extremely frightened right now. I think you have made your point."

No one knew quite what to say – anger and hurt had carried them this far, now they were beginning to feel a tad self-conscious, even a little awful, at having trampled about in the old ladies' garden and made a lot of fuss.

"The matter is concluded," Clara continued. "There will be no more letters and, if there are, then you have every right to come back to this house and politely inform the Cotterleys their behaviour will not be tolerated. But descending like this, as a mob, is not the way to go about things. You are all good, kind people, and this sort of behaviour is beneath you."

People started to glance at each other, embarrassed.

"Let us all go home and consider the matter finished."

"But what about Mr Johnson, what justice does he get?" it was the woman again, Clara tried to catch her face, but she was right at the back of the crowd.

"What justice would you have?" Clara asked. "Would you drive these ladies to suicide too?"

There was a burble of answers, mostly 'no'. The crowd began to disperse, looking a little self-conscious about their behaviour. Mr Summerton gave Clara a nod as he went past, and Oliver grabbed the arm of his father. Clara was just descending from the wall, when she spotted the woman who had raised the question of justice for Mr

Johnson. She recognised her at once as the woman from the photograph in Johnson's bureau. Their eyes met and the woman came up to her.

"I left him for another man because he was always working," she said, quite bluntly. "I don't feel good about it, but that's my guilt and shame to bear. What gave those harpies the right to harangue him about it?"

She suddenly burst into tears. Clara reached out a hand and touched her shoulder.

"You knew about the letter?"

"He wrote to me, just before…" she handed Clara a crumpled letter.

It was not very long and it largely described how sorry Mr Johnson was about everything. He also mentioned the letter the Cotterleys had written to him and the unbearable shame he felt. It was a suicide note, quite plainly. He had been saying his goodbyes to his wife and explaining his reasons for ending his life.

"I'm sorry," Clara said, knowing the platitude was meaningless.

"I don't feel good about what I did. Please believe me. I won't lie, it was all for selfish reasons and I knew it would hurt him. I am so angry, as much with myself, as those witches," she pointed at the Cotterleys' house. "Before I came here I had convinced myself he never would have done it if it wasn't for those crones prodding him. I know I am as much to blame."

She sobbed.

"I'll never forgive myself."

Clara thought that she would, eventually, and that she would move on and forget her former husband. Some of her tears seemed rather self-indulgent.

"You ought to go home," Clara said. "There is nothing you can do here."

The former Mrs Johnson patted her eyes with a handkerchief, gave a sniff, then walked away without so much as a goodbye. Clara found herself feeling even more sorry for the late Mr Johnson. She turned to Oliver.

"I have to get to the hospital. Is your father all right?"

Mr Bankes senior was sitting on a garden wall looking rather shame-faced.

"He regrets getting so cross, but he will be fine," Oliver assured her. "What are you doing at the hospital?"

"A detective's work is never done," Clara winked at him.

~~~ * ~~~

At seven the hospital opened its doors to visitors. One of them was a man in a blue police uniform. He had a bunch of flowers in one hand and a box of cigarettes in the other. He followed the crowd of relatives and friends off to see sick loved ones up the stairs, keeping to one side and trying to appear innocuous. He found himself on the second floor; the crowd was dispersing for the wards or side rooms. He walked along the corridor, gave a smile to a matron who passed, and tried to remain calm. At the door to Brompton's room he paused and took a deep breath.

The door opened inwards, blocking the view of the bed at first. As he entered, the visitor saw Brompton lying in the bed. He had bandages around his head and was tucked deep beneath the blankets. Brompton's face was invisible under all the wrappings, only a nose and mouth could be seen. A more curious man might have wondered why Brompton's whole face was wrapped up in such a fashion, considering the bump had been on the back of his head. But the man in the doorway was too anxious to notice. He crept into the room.

"Brompton, old chap, you awake?"

The patient remained stony silent. He seemed unconscious. Very carefully his visitor placed the bunch of flowers down on the bedside cabinet. He stared at the patient for a moment.

"Sorry, old man, but you couldn't keep your nose out."

The visitor slowly pulled the pillow out from under Brompton's head. Brompton snuffled a little, but didn't wake. With the pillow in his hands, the visitor hesitated.

He was about to commit murder. Enough to cause any man to pause for thought. But there was a great deal at stake, not least his freedom. If Brompton lived and reported him, then there would be no future other than a prison cell. He couldn't have that. Reluctantly he placed the pillow over Brompton's face.

"Constable Tilney, what a surprise."

Tilney jumped back from the bed and turned around. Clara was leaning against the wall, just inside the door. She had been sitting quietly in the corner of the room all the time Tilney had been plotting his actions. He had been too absorbed in his business to look around and notice her. She had only moved when he picked up the pillow, so she could block his exit.

"I came to pay my respects," Tilney dropped the pillow in haste. It fell to the floor.

"Really, Tilney?" 'Brompton' sat up in bed and started to remove his bandages. Only then did Tilney realise his error.

He turned back and saw the imposing figure of Alfie Ling sitting upright in bed, a trail of bandages sitting in his lap.

"Ling?"

"Yes, Tilney," Ling grinned. "I thought you were listening rather keenly when I was telling the boys about Brompton's miraculous recovery."

Tilney hesitated. He glanced back at Clara.

"I am just visiting," he picked up the bunch of flowers to prove his statement.

"Never knew you and James were such good friends," Ling said coldly. "Always thought you hated each other's guts."

"We had our differences, but he was still a colleague," Tilney blustered.

"Do you always attempt to smother people you visit in hospital?" Clara asked smoothly.

"I… I was rearranging the pillows," Tilney attempted a smile. "What a surprise seeing you both here."

"Let's not play games, Tilney. You are here to dispose of Constable Brompton."

"Why would I do a thing like that?" Tilney's laugh was forced.

"Because of Brilliant Chang," Clara answered him.

"Who?" Tilney didn't quite manage to make the answer sound sincere.

"I believe he has been paying you, Mr Tilney. Paying you to keep his activities in Brighton quiet."

Tilney tried the laugh again; it was no better the second time.

"What nonsense. Who is this Chang fellow? Sounds foreign."

"I think you know well enough. But, no matter, now you have been unmasked Mr Chang will have no use for you. In fact, he may begin to wonder if you will be a liability to him, rather like Brompton was."

Tilney said nothing, though the laughing smile warped to a grimace.

"How safe do you feel Mr Tilney, now that you are no longer of value to Mr Chang?" Clara persisted.

"I think I would be watching my back," Ling piped up, adding to the pressure. "I would be wondering if Mr Chang was thinking of running me down with a car."

"You are trying to scare me," Tilney managed to sound cocky, but only just.

"Aren't you scared Mr Tilney? I would be. But then, I have had a criminal come after me, thanks to you," Clara's smile was not friendly. "You enabled Billy 'Razor' Brown to escape his cell, didn't you?"

"Brown?"

"Are you going to deny you know of him too? That would be extremely foolish, seeing as he was in your police station for quite some time," Clara could see Tilney's façade beginning to crumble. "Does he work for Chang? Is that how he knew about you? Perhaps he threatened to tell everyone if you didn't release him. Brown is in prison right now, facing a rather long term of incarceration. Perhaps he would be willing to discuss the matter of your corruption for a little leniency?"

"Brown is a liar."

"Even liars tell the truth sometimes."

Tilney shifted from foot to foot. He glanced back at Ling, who had a scowl fit to melt iron on his face, then he looked back at Clara. He took a pace forward and gave an appeasing smile.

"Look, I'm sure we can come to an arrangement. Only you two and Brompton know, yes? Well, I'll give you a cut of the money I received from Chang, if you just let me get out of town. I'll never bother you again, Brompton will be safe. I'll leave the police, no one will ever hear of me. What do you say?"

"You wish to bribe me?" Clara asked coolly.

"Call it a gift, why not?" Tilney started to look a little desperate. "Look, you are right. When Chang finds out I have been discovered my life is as good as over. At least let me have a head start."

"Why would I help a corrupt policeman who allowed a thug to come after me?" Clara said, her expression cold as ice, her words hard. "Inspector, he is all yours now."

There was a medical screen tucked into one of the corners of the room. Inspector Park-Coombs emerged from behind it and stared at Tilney.

"I haven't admitted anything!" Tilney shouted.

"Do you really believe that?" Park-Coombs replied. "I think you better come with me Constable Tilney. You can explain everything in my office. Confession is good for the soul, they say."

Tilney looked grim. He threw the bunch of flowers in his hand at Clara's feet, before glowering at her.

"I wasn't doing any harm. Who cares about a few drug addicts, anyway?"

"Clearly not you," Clara retrieved the bunch of flowers. "If you don't want these I can think of a good home for them."

Ling grabbed Tilney by one arm, the Inspector

grabbed the other.

"This way Tilney," the Inspector said in a remarkably jolly tone. He was clearly quite pleased to finally have his man.

Tilney sulked, his head hung down and he looked utterly miserable. Not surprising really, considering the grip Ling had on his arm. Besides, they all knew the police were now the least of his problems. A formidable drug dealer like Chang, who could afford to bribe policemen, would not want any loose ends hanging around.

Clara watched them leave. Then she strolled along the corridor, across the staircase landing, and into another corridor. On her left she found a door marked 'Welk' and quietly entered. Mrs Welk was lying unconscious in her bed. There were no visitors, though supposedly her family had been informed of her indisposition. Clara went and stood beside her for a few moments. Then she rested Tilney's bunch of flowers on the bedside cabinet and took a pace back.

"Get better, Mrs Welk," she spoke softly, before turning and heading downstairs.

Inspector Park-Coombs had hauled his captive away by the time she arrived on the hospital steps. Instead, her eye was drawn to a big red car, clearly a sporty number, parked just in front of the entrance with its engine running. She walked down the last few steps and stared at it. Fumbling in her pocket, she withdrew the small piece of metal that had been found in the lane after Brompton's accident. She had been carrying it around idly, thinking something might trigger an idea of what it belonged to. Now she was looking at the sports car and its grand hood ornament – a woman leaning forward with winged arms stretching back. Clara held the small fragment of metal next to the miniature woman. It was identical to one of the tips of her wings.

"You like my car?"

Clara looked up and spotted Brilliant Chang. He was

dressed, as usual, in a smart suit and rakish hat. He was smoking and looked quite relaxed.

"Yes, I am," Clara smiled back. "I was just marvelling at how well your garage has fixed the damage to the front. It must have needed quite a bit of work after you collided with Constable Brompton."

"I don't know what you are talking about," Chang grinned. Unlike Tilney the accusation failed to ruffle him. He threw away his cigarette and climbed into the driver's seat of the car.

"Visiting someone?" Clara asked.

"Just keeping an eye on an old friend," Chang winked at her. "Goodbye, Miss Fitzgerald. I hope we can be as cordial as this the next time we meet."

He revved the engine, released the brake and drove off, swirling up leaves from the road as he went. A couple of people who had been about to cross the road in front of him shook their fists. Clara pocketed the small piece of hood ornament.

"Next time we meet Mr Chang," she said under her breath, "I shall make sure you are wearing handcuffs."

Chapter Twenty-Four

With the matters of Brompton and the poison pen letters resolved, there was only one question left on Clara's mind.

She paid a final call on Miss Wicks. The woman looked as sour as ever as she opened the front door.

"What do you want?"

"I assume you have heard that the Cotterley sisters were behind the nasty letters?" Clara asked. "Except yours, that is."

Miss Wicks frowned.

"You best come in," she said at last.

Sitting at the religiously scrubbed kitchen table, Clara explained the situation.

"The Cotterleys have admitted to writing all the letters, except for yours. I suspect someone else used the excuse of the other letters to send you one. The question is, who?"

"I couldn't say," Miss Wicks folded her arms across her chest.

"You cannot think of anyone who might have sent the letter?"

Miss Wicks sniffed, as if she had smelt something bad.

"No," she said.

"I know the matter is upsetting. After all, you confided the contents to Mr O'Donaghue, so you must have been concerned…"

"What did you say?" Miss Wicks interrupted.

"The matter was upsetting."

"No. About O'Donaghue?"

Clara was curious.

"He told me you had given him the letter to read, because it had arrived around the time he was laying your linoleum."

"I did no such thing!" Miss Wicks was appalled, "That little man is a scoundrel, I would no more show him a private letter than I would show it to a stranger in the street! Though," she hesitated, "he does lay lino' well, I'll give him that."

"But, if O'Donaghue knew the contents of the letter, and you did not show it to him, that means…" Clara met Miss Wicks' indignant gaze. "Why would Matthew O'Donaghue want to write you a nasty letter?"

"I couldn't say," Miss Wicks began, then she flicked her eyes to the side and grimaced. "Though, there was that unfortunate business with his sister."

"Mrs Uxbridge?"

"Yes. She made a cake for a social lunch I was hosting with the Cotterleys. It was a few years ago now. She made a sponge, but I had specifically ordered a fruit cake. Mrs Uxbridge tried to make out that I had made the error when placing the order. There was a bit of a scene. The Cotterleys and I, well, we refused to pay her for the cake," Miss Wicks twiddled her thumbs together. "Mrs Uxbridge was rather upset, but to hold a grudge all these years?"

"It was not Mrs Uxbridge who held it, but her brother. Perhaps he was even sparked by the letter she received," Clara sighed. "I shall have to have a word with Mr O'Donaghue."

"No," Miss Wicks said.

"No?"

"The matter is over and done with," Miss Wicks commanded. "And he really is the best linoleum fitter in Brighton. He is coming to do my hallway next week."

Miss Wicks shuffled in her seat.

"In any case, this business has had me thinking," she clarified. "Perhaps I was over hasty with Mrs Uxbridge all those years back and, well, I don't want to end up like the Cotterleys, despised by everyone. Maybe it is time to be a little more forgiving."

"If you are happy with that," Clara said.

"I am," Miss Wicks nodded her head firmly. "I am. Thank you, Miss Fitzgerald."

Clara was satisfied the matter was settled. She said her farewells to Miss Wicks, hoping that some good might have come from this letter business after all. In any case, she was very relieved it was all over. She set out for home.

~~~ * ~~~

It was good to have everything back to normal as they sat down for Sunday lunch. Oliver Bankes was looking much happier now his father had calmed down and was no longer being ordered to leave town by disturbed old crones. As he helped himself to Annie's best beef gravy he was smiling and talking about his latest batch of photographs. He was thinking of organising an exhibition in the summer. Clara was all for it, as long as there were no pictures of her on display.

"I wouldn't dare," Oliver grinned at her. "A portrait of you would overshadow all the others, and no one would want to look at anything else."

Clara blushed so red she looked like a beetroot and Tommy could not resist laughing. Annie kindly changed the subject.

"What is the news concerning Constable Tilney?"

"The Inspector interviewed him last night, apparently it was quite a long chat," Clara answered, relieved to be on safer ground. "He sent me a copy of his report this morning. According to Tilney, it all began around a year ago. Tilney has a taste for fine living that is not accommodated by a constable's wages. He had fallen severely into debt and was looking for any means to claw his way out. Then he met Brilliant Chang. It happened while he was visiting a dance hall with a girl. He had been spending rather freely to impress her, and when the bill arrived he found he couldn't pay. Chang spotted an opportunity. How he learned Tilney was a policeman we don't know, but that piece of information would have been easy to come across. He stepped in, splashed money around, and paid off Tilney's debt. After that, it was child's play.

"Tilney couldn't pay Chang back at once. Chang played the true gentleman and said it was not about the money, he merely wanted to help a fellow in distress. They became friendly. Chang always seemed to be at the places Tilney spent his free time. Chang had plenty of money and once, or twice, he helped out Tilney again. Before long the constable felt indebted to his new friend.

"Then the first 'favour' came. It was a minor one. Chang had been caught speeding in his car and was facing a court hearing and a fine. Would it be too much to ask, he proposed to his new friend, if Tilney could 'lose' the paperwork on his case? After all, he was only speeding a little and what was such a small favour between friends. Chang didn't need the bad press the hearing would cause, you know how people get when a foreigner appears to do something wrong, and he promised, whole-heartedly, he would never speed again. What was the point of him going to court anyway? If it made Tilney feel better, Chang would pay the amount of the fine to him, to do with it what he wished. Perhaps there was a police fund Tilney wanted to support? Or a charity? Surely that would make things even?

"No doubt Tilney was well-plied with alcohol before the request was made, and he agreed. The money was handed over and that was when it all started to go wrong. Tilney 'lost' Chang's papers, but instead of giving the money to charity he used it on himself. And once it was gone he wanted more. He was caught in Chang's snare before he knew it. After that the requests came more often – could Tilney lose a charge sheet concerning a friend of Chang's? Could Tilney listen out for news of when an arrest was happening and let Chang know? Could Tilney overlook Chang's being caught dealing drugs? And so on it went. Tilney dug himself in deeper and deeper, until Brompton stumbled across something.

"Brompton had been patrolling one night when Chang was arrested for dealing drugs. Brompton had seen the arrest made and the paperwork being written up. So he was surprised when Chang simply walked free afterwards. He went looking for the paperwork and found the same file I did. It must have shocked him to discover Chang's record ceased after 1910. He dug a little deeper, talked to fellow officers, and quickly realised that papers had been going amiss. Tilney had been none too subtle, it was only because the police were so undermanned and overworked that no one else had noticed. But Brompton was an old intelligence officer from the war, and he quickly spotted a pattern to the losses. He was putting a case together when he slipped up.

"Tilney spotted him in the archives one day. He was browsing the Chang file, but put it away quickly when Tilney approached. Tilney knew Brompton had been asking questions and he began to panic. He contacted Brilliant Chang and a plan was hatched. Chang would run Brompton down while he was on patrol. He hoped to kill him, but Brompton survived. However, he realised his life would still be in danger if anyone believed he remained a risk to Chang's operation. So he played dumb; he acted as though he had lost his mind, even taking a menial job in the hospital. All the while he was biding his time and gathering evidence. When I came to him, he wasn't sure if I could be trusted or not. I might have been sent by his enemies to see if he remembered anything. Feeling desperate, he asked Ling to get him into the archives to examine the files. He was close to having a case against Tilney, but needed to tie everything together. Unfortunately Ling had to go tend to the boiler and Tilney stumbled across Brompton. He struck him again, hoping to finish him off."

"How is Brompton?" Tommy asked.

"Recovering. Now it is clear he has not lost his mind, it is hoped he will be able to return to the police. Inspector Park-Coombs is very grateful to him and I have no doubt he will be considered for the detective role he always aspired to."

"And Alfie Ling was not a crook after all," Annie mused.

"Yes, you will have to revise your opinion of him."

Annie pulled a face.

"I suppose we can all be wrong sometimes."

They were just delving into a baked apple cobbler with fresh cream when the doorbell rang. Annie went to answer it, and returned looking a little sour-faced. Agatha was behind her.

"I do apologise for interrupting your lunch," Agatha said. "But I am due on the train within half an hour and I just wanted to thank you for your hospitality and help."

"Not a problem," Tommy grinned. "How is Mrs Welk?"

"She is awake and the doctor's think she will live. I only hope the scare will make her think twice about changing her drug preference," Agatha grimaced at her own humour. "I have been thinking about my next book. I won't be setting it in Brighton after all."

"Oh, what a shame." Clara said.

"However, I do have an idea about the main characters. A man and a woman this time, a detective couple working together, and one ought to be called Tommy, I think."

Tommy grinned from ear to ear. Annie glared at her bowl of cobbler.

"Now, I must go catch my train. Oh, by the way," Agatha dipped into a large bag she had draped over one arm and produced a book in a brown wrapper. "My first novel. I hope you enjoy it. Good day everyone."

With that she was gone. Clara pulled the wrapper off the book.

"The Mysterious Affair at Styles," she read.

"Sounds like one for the great Clara Fitzgerald to solve," Tommy said, beaming gleefully.

"I'm sure this fellow on the front cover can solve it all by himself," Clara tapped a finger on the book cover. "I'll stick to the mundane mysteries of Brighton."

"And when have any of your cases been mundane?" Tommy couldn't help but laugh. "Honestly, Clara!" he shook his head in mock remonstration. "Pass the apple cobbler, old girl."

Printed in Great Britain
by Amazon